Julian's Windows

A Modern Love Story

Michael J Spyker

AgapeDeum

Published in Adelaide, Australia by AgapeDeum
Contact: agapedeum.com

ISBN 978-0-6486957-7-6

This edition published in 2020

Publication assistance by Immortalise
Cover design: Ben Morton

Thank you Jeanne Spyker Hardy
For writing *Seagull Boy* and your descriptive insights
on the education of children with intellectual disability.

FOREWORD

The Revelations of Julian of Norwich are about love. A modern love story is a good way in which to make her insights relevant. In their original form these may sometimes be difficult to grasp. Julian's ideas are derived from mystical visions. Her spiritual theology aligns well with Scripture. Thomas Merton considered her to be one of the foremost theologians ever to live in England. She lived in troubled Medieval times and knew suffering. Her many questions Jesus answered graciously and often quite incredibly. Julian shines a special light on the divine plan for our world.

In *Julian's Windows* the anchoress has a minor but significant role. This modern love story is about ordinary people – their struggles and achievements. In the end, Lady Julian has the final word.

Michael J Spyker
Adelaide, South Australia

PART ONE

1

WHILE PUMPING OUT the bass line of *Dark Daisy* he had Georgia on his mind. That thought soon dissipated when the music demanded a bass solo. It had to be hard hitting and imaginative. The vibrant and dark energy Nick projected through the music corresponded with how he had felt for a long time now – bordering on depression and sometimes still emotionally raw. Playing bass guitar diminished his always lingering hurt. His fingers creating those low notes, it was like spitting out dark matter and the sucking in of a soothing sensation. With the bass he felt less split up into parts. Enter the zone and the music would take over. Rule everything within him. Today, that zone was on offer. Perhaps the thought of Georgia made it happen. Or subliminally Helen. Nick couldn't tell and gladly took the ride. This balm for the soul, when it came knocking, lifted his spirit.

Vorque drove the mood with superb work on his guitar. Finding the balance between the anger of metal and the intricacies of jazz. Doing justice to both was always difficult. The purist in either genre tended to consider the idea questionable. Vorque didn't care.

Neither did the audience diminished in subdued lighting. They applauded with enthusiasm. Music had kept Nick sane of late. The invitation to join *M-Jazz Indigo* at the age of almost forty was a stroke of fortune.

Famous with the metal crowds, and now rich from a disbanded grunge band, Vorque had conceptualised their style. A blend of metal, jazz and blues. With Aluka on the piano and Mr. Chen at drums there was every chance of success. *M-Jazz Indigo* had become Vorque's ambition in a niche market. He no longer performed in black leathers. Some fans appreciated the transformation, many others did not. It was early days knowing how large the number of fans might become. The audience tonight identified well with the music. It was hard hitting, modern, sensitive and intelligent. Nick pinched himself for his good luck in ever meeting Vorque. *M-Jazz Indigo* was the silver lining on the cloud of his struggling mind.

The woman was not quite drunk. Or she must be a good drinker and a little flushed. Nick understood alcohol, how it worked your body and emotions. Standing next to him at the bar she silently offered an invitation. Unlike a trophy queen. Not ever would Nick rubbish an approach like this understanding loneliness only too well. The desire for intimacy, however fragile. But he was not interested. Since Helen, he had no heart in the physicality of a woman. Well, not until recently. He smiled accepting her compliment about the music. She began a pleasant conversation about jazz, quite knowledgeable, which was fine. Nick was proficient in the genre though no expert. His feeling for the bass, for the intentions of jazz, and his vast experience with metal, qualified him for his job. He kept the discussion going out of kindness. This bar companion with her blue demeanour was good company and attractive. Her chemistry was difficult to ignore. But soon he excused himself and made it back onto the stage. There was one more set to play in this club in Soho, London. So far away from his home in Australia.

Lately, Nick had Georgia on his mind. Not replacing Helen, who was always obscurely present. He missed Helen every day still. Had contemplated suicide once, but she would not let him. Or rather, he could not get himself to dishonour her like that.

***

When Nick was almost thirty Helen had suggested they marry.

'How could I possibly marry you,' he had objected. 'I'm a musician, got no money.'

'I know about your money,' she replied. 'But don't be such an alpha male. I want you for myself.'

'You've got me for yourself.'

'I want you properly for myself.'

His reluctance to live mostly on her wages was swept aside with the suggestion that he should swallow his pride. Once married, it would become their money rather than hers. As a chemist, she was earning plenty.

'I love you Nick. I need our relationship complete. We belong together.'

Helen wiped blond hair away from her pretty face. Looked at him straight. Her eyes were misty, searching and vulnerable. All his objections melted away, instantly.

They were married in church. The members of his band entertained the guests with acoustic music, quite unlike their usual repertoire. Good musicians they were, it took little effort. They enjoyed the day as much as anyone. A married Nick was an idea for the band to get used to. But then, of late he had spent much of his time with Helen anyway. She was oaky and liked their music. Helen would never obstruct their plans, Nick had insisted.

Born with a happy disposition nothing fazed Helen overly much. Her work, she was imminently suited for. In company, she was always fun. Her main interest was spirituality in which she read widely. On weekends she relaxed together with Nick when his gigs allowed it. Went to the markets or town. Home was a terraced house in Melbourne not far from the CBD. Entertainment options were plenty.

Practical, light-hearted and up-beat, Helen managed

to pull her musician up from his moods more often than not. Moods were acceptable, to a point. Overstep that mark, though she had no real idea where to draw the line consistently, and Nick was told to buck up. Always with a smile. Though more proactive than Nick, she needed him badly. Helen understood her ability to count for naught, unless they could remain in love. With issues, they had learned to communicate properly. Out of sorts, it was soon made up. They had great years together.

'Found a new friend,' Helen declared. 'Julian.'

At home they were sitting together in a comfortable settee.

Nick raised his eyebrows in surprise. It was unusual for Helen to make male friends.

She gave him a little grin. 'I did so, you know,' she reiterated. Aware how he was taking the information.

'Why?'

'Because, I need that kind of friend.'

'What for?' Nick began to dislike this conversation.

'Oh Nick, don't worry.' Helen was amused about this show of male sensitivity. 'The name is Julian. But she's a woman. Lived during the Middle Ages.'

After a moment Nick cottoned on. 'You bought a new book?'

'Yes, wonderful. Not that you would take an interest.'

'What about this lady?'

'She was a mystic in Norwich in England. During the fourteenth century. She got sick and had visions of Jesus, which she explained theologically.'

'Trust you to find her.'

'It's beautiful Nick. All will be well, and all manner of things shall be well. When all seems lost, that is. It's what the Lord told her.'

Nick just nodded affirmatively. He respected Helen's enthusiasm, but didn't join in. His faith never reached such lofty heights. The book lay on a side table next to the TV, which only now he noticed. It became more important to her than he could have ever imagined.

Increasingly, Nick and his musical friends became better known around Australia. Their band received invites interstate and gigs that were more lucrative. A few albums they released helped that process. The downside was the increased travel, being away from home. Helen never complained. She knew this was part of the deal and was happy for Nick. He in turn made sure to be really home when at home. Create as much of a celebration as possible once together. His income improved, though it remained unpredictable. Their only regret was the apparent inability to have children. One day that would need looking into.

Then, the bottom fell out of everything. Helen was

diagnosed with cancer and had three months to live. Nick left the band. They replaced him with a hired musician. He knew though that he wouldn't be back. For the first time ever he saw Helen depressed. But not for long. Life was an interim existence to her. It simply had become a lot shorter than expected. Her main concern was Nick. He worked hard at being supportive. Took effort to not emotionally disintegrate. It became the worst time of his life.

The progression with the illness followed the usual script. A visit to the doctor for an answer to pain. It didn't seem anything alarming. Then the shocking news. Initial unbelief preceded horror realization. Followed by fast deterioration. The first few weeks Helen submitted to chemotherapy, but it made her sick. Asking the doctor whether it really was of any help, she learned that it might prolong life for a while. Nothing was certain. It's no good, Nick, she had conceded. Better to let matters take their course naturally. She had no problem with that. But the decision that hardly registered with him. In deep grief, reality had become a blurred sensation for Nick. With the occasional moment of clarity about how beautiful a wife he had been lucky to find. Though really, it had been Helen who picked him out to be the one. He well knew it and now was losing her.

Increasingly, Helen focused on Julian - the book she bought a year ago.   Many crosses and underlined sentences began to mark the pages. As she grew physically weaker her spirit seemed to find release into a reality inaccessible to Nick. Helen talked about its beauty to let him know that she was fine. Not expecting Nick to understand. It would be impossible in his state of mind. She was particularly enthralled with the familiarity of God. Lady Julian had experienced it by grace. Helen discovered it also. The kindness of God became her joy in spite of her suffering. It was beyond what Nick could comprehend. Finding no kindness in the destruction of the person he loved. If anything, it made him angry. His sole comfort was that Helen seemed unperturbed about her illness apart from the pain. She became hospitalised and deteriorated fast. Near the end, in a lucid moment she said, Oh Nick, don't have me worry about you, hey? By then she could hardly speak and was unable to read. But the book of Julian remained on the bedside table. Helen was adamant that nurses should leave it there. She held it occasionally, being in a world of her own. Finally, Helen slept away, simply and gently.

Nick took the book home. After the funeral he went on a bender, was stupefied by alcohol for a week. Helen's last words, he had no idea that they would be the last when spoken, rambled through his exhausted mind. Oh Nick, don't have me worry about you, hey? He quit the band regardless of his friends' protestations. They understood it to be best. Nick could not possibly do their music justice right now. Eventually, Nick picked himself up somewhat. He decided to leave Melbourne for country living. Find some solitude. Whether that was wise, a solitary existence, he had no idea about. For now, it seemed the right action to take. Helen's books he boxed up to be stored. Wherever he would end up, there would be a place to keep them safe.

2

AT A SPECIAL SCHOOL in Liverpool, Sr. Julian spent time with Alex today. The child was a loner and preferred to be without company surrounded by his loves: Alice in Wonderland, Jumbo, other books and DVDs. Sometimes he would welcome her into his space. Then Julian could communicate through Intensive Interaction. She would need to get down on the floor besides his cushions. When Alex invited her to 'talk' it meant he was happy and relationally in need. He was a nice looking boy of eight and capable of many things but without speech. His autism had not left him without personality though. His life simply was completely different from that of children in general. The challenge with intellectually disabled children was trying to figure their inner world out. What it was like. Why they were acting and responding as they did. What threats they experienced in their environment. For it activated certain behaviours. Presently, Alex was at ease. He peered closely into Julian's eyes and made his unintelligible sounds. Julian repeated those echoing his speech and making his language hers. She introduced a new 'word'. Spoke it louder and repeated it. With a big grin on her face she tickled Alex's nose. He joined the conversation by copying the new word sound and made gestures. Those Julian copied in turn. Together they communicated and Alex remained happy.

'Julian, please,' a voice spoke urgently. It was Lindy, who gave educational support. She had been helping Edward with his arithmetic in its most basic form. Julian got onto her feet quickly and began to talk to Edward. He had his arms around Lindy's chest and was squeezing painfully hard. Julian knew from experience how that would hurt. Edward always liked to hug a female teacher. He was best kept at the other side of the desk when teaching. But he was quick. Sometimes too quick. It was essential not to fight him for then he would press even harder. Edward was very strong. Stay calm, puff out your chest to protect your ribs from breaking and quietly call for assistance. For Edward to let go, he needed to be distracted.

'Did you see Liverpool on TV yesterday, Edward? Come tell me about it. What happened?' Julian asked him.

He looked at her with a new interest in his eyes. Liverpool was his team. He could sing the world famous line "you never walk alone" and loved it.

'Let's sing,' Julian suggested.

He let go of Lindy, who calmly moved away with tears in her eyes. She would need to fill out an incident report. Julian and Edward began to sing the Liverpool club song. That one line, repeated many times.

Edward was a challenge. But that was part of being a special education teacher. Julian taught in a Catholic school for children with disabilities. She simply loved her job. The children were special and, if you could but open your eyes to it, so different and interesting. Finding ways in which to help their development was challenging. Some would be able to find work when older. If suitable employment was available. For others that possibility would remain forever closed. Many people felt quite uncomfortable when facing people with disabilities. Julian found it unfortunate. God's goodness filled all his creatures. God's works and endlessly overflows in them all. That is what Julian of Norwich had understood from her visions hundreds of years ago. That divine goodness surely would be present in children with disabilities.[1]

Sr. Julian lived as a religious in a local community. It was part of an active order that focused on doing the work of the Lord in society. It could mean many things. For her, it was special education. At the end of teaching time, Julian wiped her hands on her jeans. In a comfortable top and trainers she didn't look anything like a religious sister. Not like what many people still generally expected. She walked to where the school bus was waiting. This morning, Stevie had come off the bus agitated. Not even his favourite bird book could engage him. He had remained free of class activities. Rocking himself into peace while hugging his quilt he had declined all interaction. Now climbing into the bus for home it seemed no better. Julian learned later, that his family had been moving house. Boxes everywhere, leaving Stevie utterly confused. He could not express his frustration and withdrew into himself. Julian thought to write a story about this beautiful boy one day.

Her own way home was by bus. A short trip through the city streets. She reflected on how the idea of becoming a religious sister had arisen about thirteen years ago. Soon she would have to make up her mind, once again. Whether to remain in the order or take her leave. That question needed answering about every three years.

She recalled how one day at primary school, she had seen a picture of Jesus suddenly come to life. She would have been eight years old. Jesus seemed to look at her, smile, and was ever so friendly. Like someone you could trust completely. It had lasted only seconds, but she would never forget. The encounter had been real, absolutely. She had kept those moments a secret, ever since. A treasure all of her own.

Her parents never found out. Emotions were little discussed even now. Childhood had been uneventful. She had been well cared for by parents with few ideas about children's needs beyond food on the table. Plus clothes to wear and doing as you're told. The home had managed to remain ahead of the bills. The quality of their marriage was never great. Dad was an authoritarian. Mother tried to keep the peace. But whatever the friction, dad had never objected to his wife's Catholic beliefs. He never intervened in their children's education. Brother and sister became well acquainted with Sunday Mass and were enrolled at a church school.

During her teenage years, particularly earlier on, she had prayed every single day before going to sleep. Simply because it was helpful. Daily, she had discussed her life with Jesus. These prayers were part of how she lived. With adolescence that habit began to gradually disappear. Once at university, her Christian activity involved no more than attending Mass on Sunday. Not every weekend. Time for the spiritual side of life came at a premium once moving into student digs. Busy with study and working a job in a pub.

In her second year, she had fallen in love with Mark. An intense relationship that lasted for months. After which he had dumped her. Her friends had bounced back quickly from those situations. It seemed the norm. But she got deeply hurt and had decided on a brief holiday, indulging her interest in medieval architecture. Just to lift her lagging spirit. The city of Norwich had become her destination. The old part of town with its cobbled stones and many ancient buildings. Great for meandering.

She should visit Norwich again one day, Julian reflected. She shifted closer to the window of the bus. Someone was taking the seat next to her. The bus smelled of damp coats because of drizzly weather.

She remembered how the River Wensum wound itself through the city just as it had in the Middle Ages. When Norwich was the second largest settlement in England. A major centre of commerce. Norwich Cathedral had been special and pivotal in determining her future. She had no idea of that when stepping through the door. Into the high space of massive Norman columns and arches that shaped the ceiling. Everything was bathing in the diffused light of enormously tall stained glass windows. For a university student with an aching heart the church had been a haven. A great place in which to sit quietly in the presence of God. The majestic surroundings had their effects on her spirit and highlighted what she well knew. The Christian side of life was slipping downhill fast. This awareness came in a kindly manner, without accusations or feelings of guilt. A vague question began drifting through in her mind. Too vague to be put into words. It had to be left alone.

Upon leaving she was asked whether having visited the largest church in Norwich, she would care to see the smallest one. It originated from medieval times. One of the greatest English mystics had been an anchoress there. A pamphlet with information gave directions.   Down

King's Street and Julian's lane. Well within walking distance. Soon the little church came in sight where Julian of Norwich (1342-1423) had lived out her life reaching the incredible age of around eighty. In days when most people were lucky to survive beyond thirty. Not much of Julian's history was known. The last thirty of her years were spent, enclosed in the cell that was attached to the little church. Where she meditated on visions received during a severe illness years before. The small space of about nine by eleven feet was spartanly furnished in medieval style. It had a positive feel though. Featuring a door and three narrow windows. One gave a view into the chapel towards the church altar.

For a person with a broken heart the chapel had been peaceful. Ideal for reflection. Thoughts about ultimate reality had come to mind. What was it all about? How did life really work, when illusions were stripped away? These questions became highlighted that afternoon. She had visited the Julian Centre as well and left with a handful of bedtime reading – interesting stuff.

The next day in Norwich Cathedral it became obvious that her life had become pretty mediocre. Defying her idealistic tendencies. In deep reflection Julian knew that for her life to have true meaning, a cause needed to be found that was larger than her. Well beyond life's mere existential focus. It needed to be a worthwhile cause, the very best. At that moment the answer was simple. In how you just know a certainty. But the consequences would not be so. The vague question from her visit to this cathedral yesterday had become clear.

Sr. Julian looked out of the window of the bus. Into a street full of commuters. At the next stop she would disembark. Yes, the question had become clear in that cathedral. A question from her teenage years. Would she become a nun? She had wondered whether the bad experiences with Mark made the idea resurface. But what she had felt in Norwich Cathedral had been far too profound for that to be the case.

Her visit to Norwich had been full of interest and encouraging. The meaning of life sharpened up that week. With her heart on the mend she had shouldered her backpack. Back to her digs and university. Whatever the future might hold, finish your education first, she had told herself. Take your time. But return to prayer. Of a kind that intimately connects with the Lord.

Sr. Julian stepped off the bus with a smile on her face. Drizzle was descending. Entering an order had taken a while. It is preferred for applicants to have lived well in society before committing to a religious vocation. But that was years ago now, her becoming a sister. The question was: would she remain one?

3

THE WELL MAINTAINED DIRT TRACK wound over a gentle hill towards a cattle farm. The morning was cold with the chill of a mild fog in the air. Nick drove his single cab four-wheel drive with loading tray slowly into the yard and stepped out into a sharp wind. The last gasps of winter.

The farm house was a comfortable brick building with many years of history. The door of a lean-to, possibly an office, opened. A man in his fifties, who Nick presumed to be the farmer, stepped out with the unhurried gait usual to those working the land. He assessed his visitor with a keen eye. Nick's pony tail, new Akubra hat, and wiry body.

'G'day,' he said genially and offered a handshake. Farmers tended to be reserved and usually friendly. This man was no different.

He noticed the tired look in Nick's eyes. A grown-up man perhaps at the edge of a downer but not quite. Some steel in the soul yet, the farmer concluded. This might be his new neighbour.

'Hi,' Nick responded, 'I'm your neighbour. Thought

I'd say hello.'

'Living in old Dave's place.'

'Yeah.'

'Cattle not bothering you?'

'No, nothing of the sort.'

The place Nick was renting with an option to buy featured an old house and about 40 acres of meadows. It used to be a dairy, way back. The farmer leased the land of the owner for grazing.

'Good.' The comment was followed by a moment of silence. 'You're new around here.'

Nick nodded. He tried to adapt to the pace of the conversation. Slow by Melbourne standards. The last few weeks, since settling near Merton in country Victoria, he had become better used to it.

'Come in for a coffee. My name is Charles.' The locals called him Chump. Those who knew him well. A legacy from his childhood days. Not for this stranger to know.

'Nick.'

Leaving their boots outside on the covered veranda, Charles ushered his visitor through a different door into a large kitchen. The Aga cooking stove, well stoked-up with wood, was burning hot. Soon Nick had a steaming mug of decent coffee in front of him on a large dinner table. But for the farmer, there was nobody around. A few questions about the cattle business were answered kindly enough. Faced with a townie, Nick's host left his own questions alone. It was not the country way to be overly inquisitive. At least not openly so with those who have no history here. Soon, Nick stated the real reason for his visit, apart from becoming acquainted.

'Where might I find a dog, for company?' he asked. 'Preferably a kelpie.'

The question received a keen look. An assessment of character. Nick, who managed to return the gaze steadily, wondered about this reaction.

'Might know of one,' the farmer admitted taking his time. He seemed to weigh matters up. 'Had a dog before?'

Nick nodded. 'As a boy.' He had grown up with Prince, their Labrador.

After a brief moment the man stood up without a word. He stepped outside and left Nick to empty the last of his coffee. The kitchen, though originally old, was well equipped. Modern furniture that included a flat screen TV. Nick noticed how little it had in common with his own much simpler place.

When the door opened again, letting in a blast of cold air, the farmer requested Nick's company outside. Sitting obediently was a beautiful brown kelpie. Fully grown and not old. 'Free, girl,' the farmer said and the dog was all over Nick, who greeted the exuberance with joy. He ruffled the kelpie's head with both hands. The chill of the veranda tiles penetrated through his socks. But he never noticed. The owner observed the scene keenly. Dogs are smart, this one definitely so. It seemed to relate well to this stranger.

'Sit,' was the short command. The kelpie obliged.

'What's her name?' Nick asked, sliding into his boots.

'Nutty.' And after a moment: 'I've forgotten her breeding name, never use it.'

The farmer gave Nick another searching look and seemed to come to a decision.

'I'm hesitant about this, because she's my father's dog,' he explained. 'Just recently he moved into a nursing home and won't be back.'

Nick understood and wisely said nothing. No point in offering platitudes.

'Thing is: I've got no use for her. She is ideal for sheep, but I only run cattle. Dad used to have sheep years ago. Very much loved the kelpie breed. He bought her for company when becoming too old for proper farming.'

'I can buy her off you?' Nick asked.

'No, you can have her.'

Before Nick protest to this surprising offer, a raised hand silenced him.

'It's simple, really. If she doesn't like you, she'll be over the fences and back here in a flash. I will tolerate that once. For dogs need to become familiar with a new home and may wish to check out the old one. If she returns twice, she'll stay with me. Experiment over.'

Nick could see the wisdom of that. He would not be interested if the kelpie had to be retrieved. They shook hands, Nick expressing his gratitude. It was grudgingly accepted.

'She loves to travel in your tray unless it rains heavily. Just hold your car door and say "up".'

When Nick followed through on the instruction the dog became confused. It looked at the farmer wondering. 'Free, girl,' he said firmly. Immediately, Nutty jumped up taking her place behind the cabin. She stuck her head around the corner and looked ahead. Her tongue was hanging out in expectation. Nick briefly ruffled her head before taking his seat.

'You will need to secure her with a lead next time,' the farmer advised. 'It's law these days. Too many hurt dogs.'

Nutty's excited face was partly reflected in Nick's outside mirror. Brown eyes and wet nose, bravely set against the wind. The dog might not have been driven about like this for a while, Nick figured. He refrained from switching on Black Sabbath. The sound of metal music didn't fit a misty countryside. The dripping wet foliage of the trees and bushes encouraged a different mood. Nutty barked once for no obvious reason but pleasure. Feeling better that morning than he had for a long time, Nick headed for the butcher shop. He needed bones and meat for his new companion.

*****

After Helen's funeral and his week of stupefaction, Nick had stayed with his older sister. She encouraged him to take a new hold on life, however feebly. He had loaded his acoustic guitar, laptop and some clothes into the car, plus a file of documentation. His sister would take care of Helen's wardrobe. Everything else could be stored up until Nick decided what to keep and what to dispose of. The front door of the place in which for years he had been so happy, he pulled shut for the last time. Determined never to see it again. It was, in a senseless way, as if the house was to blame for his misfortune.

Attending to the administrative consequences of his sudden thrust into singlehood he could only manage a few stiff drinks to dull the pain. Nick discovered that Helen had taken out life insurance well before her illness, a very significant sum. At first he baulked at that idea. Didn't want to know of it. Being rich because Helen had died, it seemed blood money. He almost threw his whiskey glass against the wall. In time remembered that he was at his sister's. Once calmed down a little tears ran down his face again. He thought they'd all been shed and felt completely gutted. Had done so for many weeks now.

He needed to get away from Melbourne, from the whole sorry mess.

As children, their parents had taking Nick and his sister on camping holidays in the foothills of the Victorian Alps. He remembered that majestic country of rolling hills and creeks. Of trees, lakes and mountain tops that defined the horizon. It now seemed the place to go to. Destined for Mansfield, Nick took leave of his worried sister assuring her that he'd be right – would get through. She found that difficult to believe. He was none too sure himself. It was mountains and open spaces he hunkered after. A large vista for his red eyes and exhausted spirit.

Those early weeks, careless about himself and anything else, Nick just had gone walkabouts. He stayed caravan parks and motels. Drank away his sorrows at night in bars or in private. Walks in the countryside were an antidote to his depression. But never for long. He lived on a dull edge between sanity and stupor. Hadn't touched his guitar once. One evening he sat in a dreary motel. The room as dark as his mood. Faint light outside his window giving a little definition. A whiskey glass on the bedside table. Then he heard her voice distinctly, in his mind. Oh Nick, don't have me worry about you, hey? It was the final straw. He broke down that night, well and truly. He was fully spent knowing that tomorrow all the pieces needed picking up. Enough was now really enough. He should get himself a life again. Helen deserved better.

In spite of his sombre moods, or perhaps because of it, Nick was attracted to the hill country. He decided to look for a permanent place to stay. His sister, who always was left worrying after their brief conversations, detected a different tone in his voice. A search of the real estate pages offered an old dairy for sale, or rent, near Merton. Nick found it suitable and signed a lease with a first option of buying. This place of local stone and a new metal roof was pleasant in a country way. Well situated amongst gums and elms, in green fields with a running creek. The windows were small in thick walls. The floors were polished timber. The house had two bedrooms. A kitchen/diner with a slate floor. A combustion heater in the living room. An Aga for cooking. Both badly in need of stoking up to drive the damp and chill out of the brickwork. The bathroom was simple but adequate. The whole place suffered from a lack of occupation and that during the winter weather. The wall between kitchen and living would come down Nick decided. If ever he bought the farm. He found a large a pile of split firewood on the concrete floor of the double shed. Other sheds and a cow yard were away from the house, remnants of the dairy of old. Though cold and unwelcome at present, the place felt okay. Nick signed the lease. He bought a folding chair and table. A stretcher, camping mattress and sleeping bag. Plus enough utensils to survive in comfort. The next step would be to trade his car in for a pickup.

After a week into his solitary existence two matters were decided. He needed to get his TV, fridge, washing machine, easy chair and some other handy pieces out of storage in Melbourne. Including the boxes with Helen's books. All his music equipment was to be brought up as well. He would go through the more personal possessions item by item. As they reminded him of Helen he was not looking forward to that. Whatever was unwanted could be disposed of. Nick would buy thick rugs in Melbourne, a new bed in Mansfield, and a second hand dining set. Most importantly, he should find himself a nice dog. Without company, the old dairy was too much of a lonesome place. Nick was determined not to touch the hard stuff before four in the afternoon. Then drink it within measure. It was worth a try.

4

Seagull Boy

THE SKY CRIED GENTLY. The boy cupped his face in his hands and turned it up, towards the tears, opening his mouth, licking the raindrops that fell onto his lips, and laughed quietly to himself.

He was a beautiful boy, a long lashed brown eyed boy. He lifted his arms up to the melting clouds and felt the water slide down them, soft and cold.

He heard the gulls behind him, screaming, calling him to run. That's what they were telling him and he answered in a voice only he could hear, 'Fly birds, fly birds.'

He turned and ran and shooed the gulls high into the liquid light.

His world was his dwelling place. He took it with him wherever he went. It was just big enough for him, no space for anyone.

MORNING

One day, as he dug his toes in the wet, sucking sand, and

repeated to himself the sound of the waves banging on the shore, the thunder came. He felt it batter his body, frightening him. He put his hands over his ears and whimpered. He crouched on the sand. Boom Boom it went, exploding inside his head, followed by the flashes, searing, sharp, engraving their image onto his closed eyes.

'It's okay,' she said. His sister. She cradled him and led him away. Away from the dark heavy shudder of the angry sky. He listed into her side, smelling her hair. His sister.

They trod the dunes. The grasses waved in the wind, whispering.

Whoosh, whoosh, went the sound in his head. His heart was thumping. Thumping heartbeat.

'It's okay,' she said. 'It's okay.'

Up at the house, he pushed open the beach door and scrabbled into his quilt.

Boom, Boom, he said. Boom, Boom, and his anxiety ebbed away from him. The smell of quilt blue soothed him to sleep.

NOON

He looked at the feather. He brought it close to his eyes, the rainbow lorikeet colours pulsating as he fanned the feather from the quill.

He flapped it against his mouth, tasting the soft tickle it made. He felt the air stroke his face as he danced his feather, round and round. He sniffed at it and laughed and only he knew why.

'Why does he do that?' asked his sister's friend.

'Why does he do that?' he said.

His sister and her friend laughed and he laughed too.

'Why does he do that?' he said quietly to himself as he lay down and pulled his blue quilt over his head, and dropped the feather to the ground.

AFTERNOON

His sister was reading. Curled up on the beach chair, on the sandy veranda.

He put his face in front of hers, up close.

'Fly birds,' he said. Not asking. Just telling.

She put down her book and smiled at him. 'Not now. Later when the sun goes away.'

He tugged her hand. 'Fly birds.' His eyes scanning her face, searching for her yes.

'Fly birds.' It has to happen.

'Okay.' She put down her book and took his hand. They ran into the dunes together and onto the sand. His sister stopped and watched him, his arms flapping, running and calling the gulls. Chasing, chasing, the gulls swooping and wheeling.

His sister wondered at her brother. A fragile life of

finely balanced beauty telling a story she couldn't read.

TODAY

Today he wouldn't leave his blue quilt. He wrapped it around him and rocked. He talked to himself, for his ears only. His sister tried to coax him away from his shelter. He lashed out and she cried.

'I don't understand him,' she told her friend.

This morning they had begun to pack. They were going home. The holiday was over.

His world which he had spun around him was being sliced, stored, shelved, and rearranged. The noise was different. It rose and fell in patterns he didn't recognize.

Things were moved, smells moved, sounds came and went. The air shivered as doors opened and slammed shut. Waves of movement unsettled him as he huddled in his blue quilt, flicking his fingers as he lay listening to his life being unravelled around him.

He heard the gulls, wheeling in the empty sky. Calling him. Calling for him. He pulled his blue quilt after him and ran down to the sands.

'Birds fly, birds fly,' he shouted.

He ran towards them scattering them with his flailing arms.

'Birds fly away, birds fly away,' he called.

They flew away from him, ducking and diving. He

spun around, anchored in the sand, watching them dance away on the wind.

He sat on the sand and wrapped his blue quilt around him. He watched the sand fly creep across his quilt, and felt the air ripple as it flew away.

He stood up and ran across the sand, his blue quilt billowing behind him. His sister came out of the sand dunes, calling for him. She watched him running, in his present moment, locked away from her, listening to a tune she couldn't hear, his tuning being different from hers.

When there were no more gulls in the sky, he came back to her.

'Birds gone, birds gone,' he said.

She cuddled him to her, him and his quilt, and kissed his head.

'It's okay, it's okay,' she whispered to her autistic brother.

'It's okay, Stevie, it's okay.'

***

Sister Julian re-read the story she had just finished and pressed print. She liked creative writing. It focused the mind in a special way. Stevie was depicted very well, she thought. Understanding children with disabilities was a gift, like being able to play music. Of course, you still had to be trained and never stopped learning. That was the joy about her profession as a special education teacher. She had few complaints. Complaints were not very helpful in any case for they messed with your mind. Far better it was to detect why something was bothering you. That might require a little introspection. Sufficient self-knowledge was a precious commodity and not that readily obtained. Julian of Norwich went as far as to declare that only in God could your true self be discovered for it found its origin in him, issued from him, and would find its final completion when entering heaven.[2] This thought was not unlike the idea of having a false and true self, or exterior and interior identity, proposed by Thomas Merton. The true self was always as free, was associated with God without intermediary, difficult to connect with, and unconditioned by society and personality pressures. It simply meant that part of us is always free and in contact with God.[3] Julian liked that idea and tried to keep it at the forefront of her mind every day.

Julian of Norwich and Thomas Merton, a famous monk. Two authors whose books she had taken from the university library upon her return from Norwich now over a decade ago. Upon completing her postgraduate studies and a year teaching, she had joined a religious community as a postulant. Following on, she had become a novice for two years, after which her first vows were taken. The vow required a three year commitment to the community she lived in. A group of about a dozen women. She had chosen to discard her family name to emphasise the significant way of life she was embarking on. This act had been voluntary. It was not a set requirement. In deciding to become Sister Julian, she agreed not to use her family name any longer. Obviously, the choice of Julian reflected her identification with the mystic from Norwich. Her revelations were a source of much comfort. Julian's insights on the nature of God were precisely what a religious sister could identify with. The fact that God loves and is familiar. Never points an accusing finger and is ever ready to help.

Those ideas were far removed from the guilt focused gospel of my childhood, Julian thought. Their discovery had been a joy. Not that you could do as you pleased for God's forgiveness was covering for you anyway. Paul explained that well at the beginning of Romans 6 and so did Julian of Norwich. But when owning up before the Lord with a promise of betterment, you may take your shortcomings lightly.

Every three years her vows needed renewing. The third time taking vows for life was possible. This year, at the age of thirty-three, Julian needed to decide on that option. Would it be three years or life? The other possibility was to leave the community altogether, with a blessing and no ties attached. Of late, Julian had begun to wonder about her vocation. Nothing specific, just a gentle nagging doubt. Perhaps, she should discuss it with her discernment guide. A spiritual director she met with occasionally. Still, that could wait. Regardless of her training with its demands of openness and obedience, at heart Julian remained an independent person – in the right sort of way. She believed in the privacy of her own spirit, always would, otherwise your identity could weaken. Identity disintegration is not what her Lord was about, quite the opposite. Nor would the Church ask this in any way. But the system, however well meant, might function contrary to its stated intentions. For all its sincerity, her community was simply a group of people who sought the best in accordance with set rules and a worthwhile purpose. That might involve mistakes. Quite early in her training Julian had decided that the deepest part of her heart would remain her own before the Lord.

Maintaining any kind of privacy when entering her community had not been easy. The questions of an in-depth interview were fair enough when considering what becoming a religious sister involved. It had made openness a necessity. All the same, Julian had been careful to guard her identity zealously. More so as she progressed in her vocation.

The evening was getting rather late. She looked across her spacious room that accommodated her bed, an easy chair, a desk and a prayer corner. The furniture was old but comfortable. It was time for her final prayers that would complete the office for the day. The office was a program of prayer, reading and reflection - both privately and in community with others. But before bringing this past day before the Lord in prayer and thanksgiving she would read a favourite passage by Julian of Norwich. The one that explained the familiarity of God. The anchoress had used the word homely on conveying the idea that God is very approachable and embracing.[4] Taking Paul's words to heart that we are the children of a God who may be called Abba, a word of endearment, Lady Julian's insights were scriptural. Her English was theologically very precise and originally medieval, as was the manner in which her ideas were presented. Modern translations would reflect that. The construction of the text remained of necessity of a kind that was popular in the mystic's time. It could make for difficult reading, but not so the passage on familiarity.

It is the greatest honour which a majestic king or great lord can do for a poor servant, to be familiar with him; and especially if he makes this known himself, privately and publicly, with great sincerity and happy mien, this poor creature will think: See, what greater honour and joy could this noble lord give me than to demonstrate to me, who am so little, this wonderful familiarity? Truly, this is a greater joy and delight to me than if he were to give me great gifts, and himself always to remain distant in his manner. This bodily example was shown, so exalted that this man's heart could be ravished and he could almost forget his own existence in the joy of this great familiarity.

So it is with our Lord Jesus and us, for truly it is the greatest possible joy, as I see it, that he who is highest and mightiest, noblest and most honourable, is lowest and humblest, most familiar and courteous.[5]

Julian simply loved this passage. The idea of a kind King offering familiarity and being happy to let everyone know, felt so right about Jesus. The medieval mystic, in her vision, had seen it 'bodily'. As if in real time. The Lord presenting himself as humble and courteous to his people, it made such a lot of sense. This is what love was all about, and thus God, who is love. Lady Julian was careful to explain that this familiarity remained hidden in our present life unless revealed by grace.[6] But spiritually that made little difference, made it no less real. God's familiarity could be accepted by faith, sensed as real in prayer and rejoiced in accordingly. Sr. Julian offered her final prayers for the day once again marvelling at the goodness of God. She asked for guidance regarding the renewing of her vows and felt reassured of a correct solution over time. She loved her bed and soon was sound asleep trusting in the morrow.

5

NICK DECIDED to buy the old dairy after a report by a building inspector said everything was sound. No salt damp, dry rot or structural deficiencies. The cracks were normal in brickwork and of no concern. The roof had been insulated. The only advice was to add to the run-off of the rainwater tanks, taking the overflow further away from the house. On a sunny spring day everything looked fresh and attractive. But there was work to do, much of it. The small garden needed attention. There was a large vegetable plot overgrown with weeds. A few potato plants stubbornly held on. The outside walls of the house needed patching up in places. That was only the beginning of it. Young Nick had often helped his father, who was a spare-time builder, with significant structures. That experience would come in handy. Every activity was closely scrutinised by Nutty with that sharp eye of a kelpie. Or lazy one, when almost asleep.

The evenings remained the most difficult to live through. Three months after his loss, it hit Nick hard that Helen would never be back. That reality well and truly had set in. A normal progression in grief, his sister told him. He had to drink his pain away. There seemed to be little option, but he managed to limit the damage. Asking God why this had befallen him was no longer a question. No answer would come. Though Nutty would never understand, the dog seemed to share in Nick's misfortune bravely. She never left his side and had a mat next to his comfortable chair. The sheer power of her *joie de vivre* forced him into a good start every day. Over time the hurt was easing. The state of his property improved and Nick began to think about his guitar again. Every evening in the kitchen, the place he kept warm instead of the living room, he listened to music. Mostly Black Sabbath and Opeth - the more melodious Opeth - and some rock. Also Mahler, a classical composer and his favourite. That music fitted melancholic moods well. But nothing could take the dull ache in his gut away. Keeping it subdued was the best he could hope for.

Nick visited the pub near Merton regularly. It brought a social dimension into his solitary existence. The counter meals were good. Nick didn't mind cooking. That was a positive. But eating someone else's effort and following it up with a drink was always nice. Nutty remained in the car, comfortable on the passenger seat with the windows partly down. Over time the locals came to accept this townie as a decent enough bloke. Closed up about his history, but okay. He was making a good job of old Dave's place. Merton was within two hours from Melbourne and close to the snow fields. It saw a stream of visitors every year. The pub was used to new faces.

One evening, Nick had a drink in the bar after a good steak dinner. A man stepped through the door he had not seen before. Judging by the way he moved and was dressed, he was not local, but used to cosmopolitan life. Nick, from that background himself, easily recognised it. They made eye contact briefly. It was not intentional. Nick sat at a table with his back to the wall on the other side of the room. With little to do he kept an eye out for new arrivals. The man ordered at the old bar, took a sip, and looked around. He came Nick's way.

'Mind, if I join you?'

'Sure,' Nick responded, a little surprised.

'Name is Tom.' Tom sat down across the table fully at ease.

'Nick.'

The man, a little older than himself, looked familiar. But Nick couldn't place him.

'You're not from here,' Tom concluded, 'though you look sort of local.'

'True,' Nick admitted. He took a slow sip of his drink wondering about this unexpected conversation. How best to respond.

'Sorry, Nick. I'm not nosy. Just like meeting people who seem interesting to me. In this pub, you're the one.'

'First visit?' Nick asked.

Tom shook his head. 'Few times. Own a place in the hills –a get-away.'

There was nothing surprising in that. Nick enquired where home might be.

'Melbourne. Not originally. My wife's home town.' Tom explained.

So was mine, Nick thought fleetingly and shrugged the thought away. 'You sound English,' he observed. The accent was noticeable. Australia was heavily populated by the English.

Tom smiled genially. 'Guilty.'

There was a lull in the conversation, Tom at ease and in no hurry, Nick wrestling with his reservations about talking to strangers more than superficially. He felt in need of friendship, but was reluctant. Not like the Nick of old.

'Where're you from?' Tom asked eventually.

'Used to be Melbourne. Have a place here now.'

Tom gave this handsome guy with his three-day stubble a look-over. Long dark hair in a ponytail. Eyes that were struggling to brighten up. An outdoors hat dropped on the spare seat beside him. As a practical man, perceptive and basically kind, he felt for this bloke. This sense of empathy happened to him at times. No need to reason why. Tom liked people, was an extrovert, and in his field a no nonsense operator. It had stood him in good stead.

'Want another drink?' he asked. 'Whiskey, I take it.'

Nick would love another whiskey, but had reached his quota. 'Got to drive home,' he explained. 'Soda water would be fine.'

It was his first concession towards companionship. No one had offered him a drink for a long time.

When Tom returned, carrying a beer for himself, Nick decided to open up a little.

'My wife died, not long ago,' he explained staring at the rising bubbles inside his tall glass. Nick was well aware of the subdued impression he made on people. He felt to justify it to this stranger, who took the effort of having a chat without being unduly inquisitive.

Tom didn't respond, had a good swig of his beer. He nodded in understanding. After a moment he asked whether Nick's job had been different before coming to Merton. It seemed likely and was a neutral question.

'Musician.'

'Ah.' Tom smiled broadly, in surprise. 'That makes two of us.'

Nick, looking up from his soda with awakened interest, noticed the quick shrug of Tom's shoulders. As if making an apology. This was a pleasant guy, interesting and kind. Their conversation became a discussion about music. Their preferences were alike. The longer it took, the more animated Nick became. Tom invited him to his shack, where there was a small studio in which they could have a jam. If Nick would care to come.

***

'Up girl, he ordered. Nutty jumped into the tray with pleasure. Nick needed eggs and had a special address for this. Mrs. Harms, who lived on the edge of Merton in a house with a large yard. She kept chooks for extra income and sold homemade condiments. The thought of visiting her cheered him up. Soon Nick and his dog were on their way through a countryside that was welcoming the end of spring. He never tired of the rolling hills and surprising vistas. Passing a local coming the other way Nick raised his hand in greeting. A common courtesy. Soon Mrs. Harm's place came in sight.

'Nick, come in.' Mrs. Harms welcomed him with a smile. Already at the door before he could knock. She had noticed his car entering the driveway.

Nutty was put on her lead tied to a veranda post. The dog disturbing chickens had to be avoided. She didn't mind. There usually was a treat at the end of these visits.

'Good dog,' Mrs. Harms said patting the kelpie. Nutty responded with a wagging tail.

'Kettle's boiling Nick. Time for a cuppa.' Mrs.

Harms assumed their meeting would progress as usual. Tea and freshly baked cake with cream.

Mrs. Harms observed her visitor. He seemed more at ease today, but still troubled. She liked Nick, who reminded her of her own two boys. So very male. And vulnerable once you probed a little deeper. To date, she had been careful not to do so. Her boys had long left home. One living in Sydney and the other overseas. It was a good reason for an international holiday. At her age of almost sixty that was still well possible.

Mrs. Harms was the only person to know of Helen's death, besides recently Tom. During their conversations she had asked few personal questions. Nick never mentioned the painful side of his story. Apart from his reasons for settling in the country Victoria.

'I've been harmless for almost twenty years now, Nick,' Mrs. Harms confided to him.

'Sorry?' He was about to put the fork into his mouth for another bite of cake, but stopped midway.

'It's a little joke I play on myself. When Matt died suddenly, I was left without my Mr. Harms – left harmless.'

Nick gave it a smile, this neat play of words. He had wondered about Mrs. Harms' husband, what happened to him. Another person, who had died too young. The news surprised him, but why? A Billy Joel song line, "Only the good die young," came to mind. However illusionary the suggestion.

'It would have been his birthday today.'

Nick remained silent. Mrs. Harms engaged with her private thoughts for a moment.

'I almost buried him twice, you know: Once into the ground and once in my mind. The hurt was so great, that at first I decided not to speak of him. Even think of him much. That was wrong.'

She smiled at Nick, who had stopped eating.

'Other cultures around the world are much better at honouring their dead than us. Out of sight, out of mind – so wrong.'

This was not what Nick had expected to hear from Mrs. Harms.

'But I came to my senses. Counted my blessings at ever having met Matt. Now I'll talk about him whenever suitable. Also remind my boys what a fine father they had. I still miss him. But that's life. It comes to us unannounced and as it sees fit.'

Nick had lost his appetite. These words of wisdom were hitting home. Well aware of it, Judith Harms felt a deep compassion for this suffering man. She remembered her own days just after Matt's death. The best help she could offer was a question to be asked. But first there was a comment.

'You're eating Matt's birthday cake, you know.'

Nick's mind took a little twist. This information was

stretching his sensibilities. Eating a dead man's birthday cake. How unusual was that, or was it? Was it wrong to keep the memory of a good man alive? If Mrs. Harms baked him a cake every year, not something he would do for Helen, was that really so odd? After some time, not speaking a word, Nick stuck his fork into his cake and took another bite. It tasted great.

'Tell me about Helen,' Mrs. Harms suggested. 'If you feel able to.'

Slowly Nick put his fork down. He understood that how he felt about sharing his memories of Helen was today no excuse. During the months on his own no opportunity for doing so had arisen. He would have refused. Not so now. Mrs. Harms was right. She knew how painful such talking could be. In a friendly and clever way, she had shown him his duty towards the person he loved more than anyone. Helen deserved to be introduced. What she had been like. Mrs. Harms was to be credited for pointing this out while risking his possible reaction. Haltingly, Nick took the next step on the road to recovery. He spoke more freely as his memories moved along.

Mrs. Harms was aware of what it was costing Nick. Over time talking about Helen would become easier. With enough for one day, she ended their conversation.

'Well, Helen lives in glory now. Of that we can be certain. Just like Matt.'

Nick fully agreed, always would. If only her entering that glory hadn't happened so soon. Worn out, but having found emotional release, he took his leave from Mrs. Harms. Expressed his gratitude. He drove back to the old dairy deep in thought.

***

That evening Nick cranked up the auxiliary amp of his bass guitar. He worked through a number of riffs at speed. Spitting out dark matter. His inspiration was lubricated by a number of whiskeys. Nutty was unimpressed. Fast asleep near the warm Aga.

6

AN EXCITED BARK by Nutty brought Nick through the back door onto the veranda. A farm vehicle came to a halt. Nick's neighbour Charles stepped out. Nutty was all over the farmer, who greeted her warmly, taking his time. Nick observed the scene with affection. When a dog likes a man, it showed he was a decent person. 'Sit girl,' Charles said after a while and approached Nick with a handshake.

'Mind, if I come in for a minute?'

'Please do,' Nick responded holding open the door.

Charles slid out of his working boots and entered the kitchen. He noticed the guitars in one corner, a box on the table with knickknacks and memorabilia spread out. A nice photo of a pretty woman was resting against the box. Charles had a feeling about this but didn't comment. A man was due his privacy.

'Please, take a seat,' Nick offered finding no need to explain the items on the table. 'Would you like a tea or coffee?'

Charles sat down. He thought it the polite thing to do, though his visit would be brief. He declined a drink for, he had little. But would gladly come another day for a coffee.

Nick accepted the excuse with ease. His neighbour looked troubled though he took pains hiding it. Farmers have broad backs, sometimes too much so.

'Thing is, my old man hasn't got long to go - asked to see his dog one more time.'

Nick was sorry to hear that. 'I understand,' he said. 'You're welcome.'

'Shouldn't take long. I see you're looking after Nutty well. That's good.'

The kelpie was sitting at Nick's feet with a keen eye on Charles.

'She's a great dog,' Nick said, 'thanks for trusting me with her.'

Charles didn't respond and slowly got onto his feet. The task ahead was bothering him. Taking the dog to his dad as a farewell. But it had to happen and Nutty would brighten the old man's eyes.

'Cattle no bother?' he asked. With Nick as the new owner of the old dairy the grazing arrangement had been transferred.

'No Charles, no bother at all. Glad to have them around.'

'You're okay, Nick,' Charles responded, which was solid praise from a local.

'Thanks,' Nick said and opened the door.

They walked into the yard where Charles said 'up' to Nutty. She looked at Nick, who told her 'free girl'. Nutty and sprung excitedly into the tray of Charles' car. Nick watched them drive away. He wasn't the only one facing his grief. There were plenty of others out there.

Nick brewed a strong coffee. He had decided to bring Helen out of hiding. In his mind, his conversations and from the box in which her special things had been stored. He was sorting it through. What to display and what to keep close handy. Plus the things that would remain in the box. Amongst Helen's jewellery he found two hereditary items. They should be offered back to Helen's mum. Nick had to admit to having ignored Helen's parents after her death, which was wrong. They would be hurting badly from the loss of their daughter. Engrossed in his own misery he had ignored that too much. His next trip to Melbourne would include a visit. They were nice people and had always been good to him. In spite of reservations about their daughter marrying a musician. A long haired man with an uncertain occupation. Nick put the heirlooms in a drawer of the sideboard.

An item that stirred fond memories was a picture of the Trinity by Rublev. Arm in arm with Helen, they had found it at the flee-market. Often they had visited there, just for fun. It usually was followed by lunch in one of the small eating places that are so common in Melbourne.

Helen had loved browsing. Nick decided to hang that picture on the wall near the Aga. He fetched a hammer and some nails from the shed.

There were other ornaments that reminded of Helen's faith. A faith that was also his own. Though it burned at a low flame, one he often ignored. That the flame had not been extinguished was a surprise. Nick had faced that question squarely some time ago. A necklace of round wooden beads with a cross he displayed on the wall near his guitars.

He might have displayed other bits and pieces had there been room. Nick still lived mostly in the kitchen. Various items went back into the box for later.

A picture of Helen needed a place still. Nick couldn't bear hanging it up prominently. Helen's lovely, happy face looking at him all the time. His emotions were too fragile for that. Nor did he wish to hang the photo out of sight in another room as if disowning her. There was a section of wall next to the sideboard obscured from view to most of the kitchen. That would have to do for now. He hammered the nail in carefully making sure it was firmly secured.

That left one item to consider. It was a text which Helen had printed out to be framed. The size was A5, not large, but clear to the eye. It read, in old English, *Alle Shalle Be Wele – Julian of Norwich*. Nick hesitated whether to display it. All shall be well. That was quite a statement in his present predicament. His spirit urged him to be positive. In good faith he grabbed the hammer and gave the text a good spot. It was as if Helen was smiling. While he fought back his tears. Memories of her were now visibly present in his life. Nick took a deep breath – partly satisfied, partly apprehensive. But he knew to have done right. With the step of a man determined to hold it together, he took the hammer to the shed and grabbed the axe to split some fire wood.

***

Late afternoon the following day Nick arrived back home hardly able to count his good fortune. He had visited Tom, as arranged, for a jam session. Looking forward to it, but never expecting what he was about to find out. His knock on the front door of a well maintained old farm house, was quickly answered. Tom smiled at the sight of Nick and his dog, and a nice dog it was.

'Come in,' he said.

'Can Nutty roam freely,' Nick asked. 'Or shall I put her on a lead?' He always sought the best for the kelpie.

'Sure, let her go.' Tom's lifestyle didn't allow for a dog. It was one of his regrets.

'Free girl,' Nick ordered and with guitar stepped into the house. It was typical of older buildings. A passage way through the middle with rooms leading off on either side. At the back there was a modernised kitchen. Tom, walking to the fridge, asked whether Nick would like a beer. With can in hand they moved into a big room, probably recently built. It stretched the full width of the back of the house. Large panels of glass separated the space from a covered balcony. The view was magnificent from the high end of a valley. Everything for a comfortable lifestyle was on offer. A variety of musical instruments in one corner included a baby grand. The first impression took Nick's breath away. A large framed black and white photo on the main wall drew his attention. Suddenly, Nick understood why Tom had looked vaguely familiar. In the music world he was Vorque. A famous metal guitarist known internationally.

Tom observed his visitor's surprise with amusement. He suggested they sat down at the main table.

'You are Vorque,' Nick said, just to make sure.

'No Nick - and yes.' Tom shook his head briefly, still smiling. 'I am Tom - Tom Kettleling to be precise. Vorque is a persona I created to help me in the music industry and make good money. Vorque doesn't exist in real life, not in my real life anyway.'

'You've stopped the band,' Nick said, which he knew to be true.

'Yes. That kind of life, on the road all the time, you can only do for so long. You run out of energy. Creative energy as well and to be frank, I've played enough metal by now. But I'm still fond of it.'

'What brought you to Australia?' Nick asked and remembered Tom's wife being from Melbourne. He was a down to earth guy, and smart. Besides being a fabulous musician. Tom would have spent most of his time in Europe and the USA and have interests there.

'Aluka. She is from Melbourne and suggested we should get a place there. I've added this house in the country as a get-away and for inspiration. It's close to the snow fields in winter and I like skiing.'

Nick nodded in understanding.

'Please never call me Vorque, Nick. And keep my true identity well hidden from the locals. I've shortened my long hair to make recognition less likely. In Melbourne that's hardly possible and I can live with that. In Merton, I much treasure my privacy.'

'Nice to meet you, Tom,' Nick said offering a hand indicating a deal.

'Likewise,' Tom replied, shaking with a firm grip. 'Let's do some music.'

Nick was facing a challenge he had not expected. A jam was fine, but suddenly doing it with a very accomplished guitarist changed things. He drove that thought away. Trusted in his ability, and why not? Nick knew that his skill as a bass player was a decent cut above proficient.

'I'm looking forward to us playing together,' Tom said walking towards the instruments. 'Finding someone capable of proper jamming is a stroke of luck for me. This house is a great place for music. Let's enjoy, just have fun. We'll stick with metal for now and some rock.'

Using popular riffs and progressions, Tom discovered that Nick was a fine bass player. He tested him with a piece Nick hadn't heard before, didn't know the feel of. Soon Tom had some good bass lines joining him. Time passed quickly. Tom called a halt and offered another beer. He slid a CD into the stereo and the sound of jazz began to fill the room.

In an easy chair Nick listened with interest. It was not a style of music he had spent a lot of time on. He liked its freedom of interpretation and intelligence.

'Know anything about jazz?' Tom asked.

'Miles Davis and Brubeck's, *Take Five* – not a great deal.' Nick thought honesty to be best.

'Classical music?'

'Love Mahler,' he replied.

Tom nodded in recognition. Nick's tastes in music were not one sided. With real musicians that would never be the case.

'I'd like you to do something, if you don't mind,' Tom suggested. He walked to the bookshelves and grabbed a small stack of CDs and a book.

'Take these, Nick, please. It's jazz. In a month's time

I'll be back here with Aluka. She's a jazz pianist. Let's see whether we can play some jazz together.'

The unspoken suggestion was that Nick should study up on the genre in the meantime. He would be happy to. It put a musical purpose back into his life, a very welcome development. He left Tom expressing heartfelt thanks.

'You're okay, Nick,' Tom told him.

It was the second time in two days someone had said that.

***

Nick stood on the back veranda ready to enter his kitchen. Nutty had disappeared into the paddocks. Playing jazz with Vorque, who would have imagined that? Just as well he had yesterday's left-overs for heating up. His mind was miles away from cooking any kind of dinner.

7

SISTER JULIAN LOVED LIVERPOOL. The wide waters of the River Mersey. The modernised city centre with itsfocus on the arts. It all gave her pleasure. As a postulant she had arrived in the Liverpool years ago for a job at the Talitha Cumi Special School and could only applaud her good fortune. As a religious she felt in no sense cut off from the world, or special in any way. Rather, it made her look at society with a sharper eye. One that understood the daily plight of humanity from a different point of view. There was a larger purpose at work behind everyday life than most people would recognise or could accept. The norm in modern culture was to function independently of the spiritual. That left an important part of your actual potential underdeveloped. It was a pity. Faith in a higher purpose could be a real help. The human person was a fragile creature, however much that might be covered over by convention. Circumstances could be debilitating and coping adequately a challenge. Julian was to conduct student interviews this evening. Discussing the education of a disabled child with the parents could be problematic.

Not all parents at Talitha Cumi were religious. Those who professed to be might not find strength from it. She would not to go home after work as her first interview began at six o'clock. In her favourite eatery, only a short walk away, she ordered soup of the day plus freshly baked bread. It tasted delicious.

Liverpool was best known for its football and the Beatles. Their song *Let it be*, her favourite, was quite prophetic in a way. John and Paul would have had no idea about that. 'There will be an answer, let it be!' That was exactly what Julian of Norwich had written near the end of her book. That once the mysteries of God are revealed to us, we will have to admit that God's creative designs, suffering included, were perfectly chosen to ensure the glorious and eternal outcomes God had in mind.[7] Without the present as it is, the splendid future to come would not be possible.[8] All our questions will be answered to our satisfaction and all the wisdom behind it revealed. That realisation did not make light of humanity's struggles and pains, or those of nature for that matter. But it was rather reassuring to know that everything in life did not happen without a higher purpose. You could take comfort from that. If you cared to accept the fact.

When in trouble Mother Mary comes to me, the song suggested. The mother of Jesus was Sr. Julian's favourite lady. From childhood she had been urged to bring all her problems before Mary. But ever since seeing that picture of Jesus at primary school come to life, the Lord had been the only one she would ever talk to in prayer. In Mary she was finding a disposition of character worthy of aspiring to. The Catholic tradition over the centuries had used the image of gentle Mary, meek and mild, as an example of female submission to further male dominance in the church. The Protestants ignored Mary as if of little significance. Both positions were appalling and an injustice to the Mother of God. I'm your servant, let it be according to God's word, Mary had told Gabriel upon learning she was to have a baby.[9] She had stuck to that pledge of 'letting it be' as God ordained all her life. At the visitation she had been just a young girl, only recently able to reproduce. The birth of Jesus and all that happened thereafter she kept quietly within her heart. The two times that she had not seen her place clearly was when suggesting to Jesus that miraculously he should supply some wine at the wedding at Canaan.[10] And when worried that her unpredictable son might be possessed by the devil, as suggested by the religious teachers, she had set out to find him with the help of his brothers.[11] In both cases Jesus' response had seemingly been to disown her. He had to make it clear to Mary that she should not mess with his mission.[12] From then on she had kept a low profile and ministered with other women who followed Jesus during his walk as one of the crew. At the cross a sword pierced her heart. It is highly likely that she would have been present when the resurrected Jesus appeared to his disciples in a locked room, but it is not recorded. The information Luke gathered for his Gospel probably never came from Mary directly. She might have left for heaven before Luke could seek her out. The woman who could have declared herself the Mother of God and spoken truly, had shun all recognition to avoid taking attention away from her son. She had well understood her role. What a singularity of purpose she had maintained. Mary would have been meek, but so was Moses and he was a great leader. She would have been kind for in good people hurt mellows them. All the struggles of motherhood were hers and beyond. In death she remained anonymous as there are no records of it. In heaven though there is only one person Jesus will call his mother and that is Mary. It was unjust the manner in which her legacy had been treated. Mary was the preeminent example of a person who had lived faithfully and powerfully in accordance with what life ordained. She deserved honour and recognition properly bestowed. As many of the women in the history of the church do – but that was another story.

Julian thought of Lady Julian, who had understood from her visions that Mary was so filled with grace and every kind of virtue that she surpassed all creatures.[13] As a mother she loved so deeply that her pain surpassed all others.[14] Jesus takes such a delight in her that in her honour he wishes for everyone to do likewise.[15] It was even suggested that because Mary became the channel for the unification of divinity and creation by birthing the Christ, figuratively she became the mother of all who are saved in the Saviour, while the Saviour is the true Mother.[16] This idea seemed rather convoluted. An example of a mystic gaining insights that may be difficult to put into words because the nuances of what was detected were so subtle. Whatever the case, the true significance of Mary should not to be denied.

Julian liked the idea of Jesus as Mother[17] also, the Father giving birth in His Son to the creation. The mystic from Norwich dealt with it extensively. However, it was time to walk back to school. She would meditate on the motherhood of God sometime soon, as she had done before.

When she arrived at the classroom, Paul's parents were waiting. They apologised for being early. Julian fully understood. The traffic in town could be unpredictable. It was best to plan for that. At the start of the school year a professional education plan had been designed for Paul with input from his parents. Paul had limited ability and in helping him learn new skills it was best if those were immediately relevant to his family life. Paul, with his dad and younger brother, went to the football every week and enjoyed a pie and coke at halftime. However, Paul was incapable of enjoying those goodies as one normally would. He had to be taught how to drink using a straw and how to eat a pie without spilling it all over him.

'Thanks,' dad said. 'Paul is getting better at handling his food. There is a little while to go yet, I suppose?' Is it true that one day his son might be able to enjoy his treats without any help at all? It was the unspoken question.

'Yes,' Julian agreed. 'Our occupational therapist is pleased, but things can't be hurried. Every week during our lessons in the kitchen Paul is learning. Our speech pathologist has drawn up an individualised eating and drinking plan based on what we think Paul can achieve, as you will know. It seems to get results.'

'Yes, it does,' Paul's mum agreed. 'It's a real help too.'

Paul's parents loved their son and were realists. He was severely developmentally delayed and though nine years of age functioned at the level of three to four year olds. Julian assured his parents that given more time the goals they had set for Paul would be accomplished. She had checked before the meeting with both specialists involved and received that assurance. They discussed related matters. Paul's parents were free to ask or suggest anything they felt was helpful. It was obvious that they appreciated the work of Talitha Cumi in educating their son and were willing to accept its limitations.

Not all parents were that understanding. Julian, working with their children every day, knew how difficult their parenting would be. At times she had been confronted with the suggestion that her capacity to fully appreciate that was limited. Because she was not a mother with a disabled child. That was true, but only to a point. Her training had covered those difficulties intensively. Being sensitive to relational issues, which occurred in any setting, Julian felt the perception to be unwarranted. The idea that she had insufficient sympathy for the problems the parents were facing was ridiculous.

'Why aren't you teaching Samantha to read and write? You are actually teachers, I presume.' Little eight years old Samantha's dad posed this question gruffly first off at the interview. Julian had never met him. Apparently, his job often took him away from home. His wife had persuaded him to come and now she was all tensed up. Julian knew Samantha's mum to be level-headed about her daughter's prospects.

Samantha was a happy, chatty child, who loved her special doll. Dolly was included in the teaching program that aimed at developing the social skills of sharing, being loving and kind. The managing of anger was another focus. When Dolly was taken of her by another student, Samantha would, without fail, tackle the unfortunate perpetrator to the ground. She had to learn tolerance. Dressing Dolly up helped in learning about colours. With a vibrant imagination Samantha would make her doll the central figure in role plays. In those, she protected Dolly from wind and rain or gave her a bath and a warm bed to sleep in. It all assisted in developing Samantha's caring nature.

'She's happy here,' mum intervened. 'And she's safe. I don't care whether she can read and write. It's not as if she will ever get a job.'

Julian decided not to respond to Samantha's dad as his wife had answered for her. Seemingly, this was not a new argument between them and a well-trodden path.

At the end of their child's schooling, parents could experience profound grief. Samantha's dad, with the ideas he held, was bound to be facing that. So much hoped for, so little of it coming true. Progress over the years could be slow. It meant not that all had been in vain. Every child at the school was constantly painting a different masterpiece of being human. If only that fact could be acknowledged and appreciated. It needed real patience to enter into Samantha's world. Slow down to her pace and beauty would be found. Sadly, her father had not been able to adjust to that. He would do better in taking Samantha for who she was: a worthwhile little person, beautiful but different. It was unhelpful to compare her to her sister all the time. But his frustration was understandable. Julian knew of an instance where the husband simply had left home for good, being unable or unwilling to cope. In spite of his protestations, that seemed unlikely.

Julian felt like a hot cup of green tea and brewed herself that bevy in the staff room. She had one final interview. It should not be difficult as Tara's parent understood their daughter's disability. Tara was on the autism spectrum, but with high functionality. She had been assessed as having Aspersers syndrome. Tara had once attended mainstream education for three years quite unhappily due to a lack of friends. The students had not made much of an effort to interact with her. Those who tried had been faced with Tara's poor social skills. Her inability to notice social cues, and be part of the group. Her obsessive fascination with butterflies at the expense of much else did not endear her to her peers either.

Tara, for her part, was not interested in the things the other girls of her age were busy with. Like bracelets and little notes to each other. All the giggling that was usual when young girls got together. She had cried a lot in public school not understanding why her peers were avoiding her. But things were different now. At Talitha Cumi she could access a computer and had assembled a 'Kid's guide to Butterflies.' With help from staff it was printed out and presented at assembly. Tara knew everything about the life cycle of a butterfly. The different kinds, their names and species.

The help she needed was in learning that everyone was different. She herself was different. She needed to become better at detecting and managing the nuances of relationships. One day she would enter the workforce and had every possibility of finding a partner.

As expected, her parents were full of praise. They did not consider their daughter attending a special school to be a defeat. As if Tara was receiving second rate education. They understood that only a school like Talitha Cumi could offer the necessary expertise in pedagogy. A professional understanding that was based on best practice in the field of disability. It heartened Julian, who was passionate in extolling the place of Special Schools. Her job was a good one. That could have its moments. Nothing was perfect. Not this side of the heavenly divide.

8

IT WAS THE BEGINNING of term and the day for professional development. The first hour was dedicated to spiritual reflection with input from the staff. Today was Julian's turn. She had been asked to explain her choice of name as a Sister and given it serious thought. What might be said about a visionary and spiritual theologian like Julian of Norwich while keeping it simple? Some of her ideas were unconventional. But the main theme, the incredible love of God, was not. That would be the focus of her presentation.

Julian began by telling of her visit to Norwich years ago. How and what she had come to know about the anchoress. As an ordinary citizen Julian of Norwich, at thirty years of age, had received visions during an illness unto death and survived. Her desire had been to see the passion of Christ, which was revealed to her in detail: the Saviour on the cross and what had happened to him there. Lady Julian had written it down. Buying a copy of *The Revelations* had been easy, Julian explained. Reading them was not. Not then for a young education student and it still could be difficult today. The book had spawned her interest in spiritual theology, which had encouraged her to read more widely.

The background of Julian of Norwich, her maiden name and family lineage, was unknown. Once in her cell, at the Church of St. Julian, she had taken that the name of that saint name for herself. She would have been around fifty years of age with another thirty to live. Her visions had been written out soon after their occurrence, when the mystic was still a common town dweller. Once in her cell, Julian had meditated on them more deeply. It urged her to write out a longer text on how she understood her visions.

When becoming a Sister, I had the option of keeping my family name or to change it, Julian told the staff. I felt to identify with the person whose ideas about God had come to mean so much to me.

'What is your real name then?' a male teacher asked.

'That's just for me to know,' Julian answered with a smile.

'Probably, Susan,' another suggested.

'Close, but that's my mother's name.'

'Will you guys please shut up,' one of the female staff suggested.

Julian didn't mind the banter. The staff, they were a good group. She continued her talk.

Julian of Norwich is the best writer I have come across in expounding the suffering love of God. The idea that God sits in the sky being unaffected by human affairs, but for his Son suffering on the cross, is incorrect. For centuries though that thought has held sway in theology. Following the notion of the Unmoved Mover found in Aristotle's philosophy. Julian of Norwich shows that nothing could be further from the truth. And other visionaries agree. Let me read you an insight recorded by Teilhard de Chardin. On the battle grounds of Verdun during the First World War a soldier friend of Teilhard, the man was soon to die by enemy fire, told him of a vision. It gave the soldier peace in such horrible circumstances. He was in a church and looked at a picture of Christ giving his heart to people. From the looking, a vision slowly began to emerge and develop. He saw the magnificence of the Eternal Christ whose appearance kept changing. At the end the soldier was allowed to stare deeply into Christ's eyes. Let me read those sentences to you, what the man saw.

> And I stood dumbfounded. For this final expression, which had dominated and gathered up into itself all the others, was indecipherable. I simply could not tell whether it denoted an indescribable agony or a superabundance of triumphant joy.[18]

Julian read the paragraph out twice and reiterated that it

was not Christ on the cross the soldier saw, but the Eternal One. From the eyes of Jesus, he must have understood that the Saviour suffered the pain of the whole world while rejoicing in his complete victory over the primary force behind it all: sin. I imagine that the soldier no longer felt deserted in battle for Christ was present in his suffering and that of others. God's suffering love was upholding the whole world, the universe even. Perhaps Teilhard's friend understood what Julian of Norwich had been told by the Lord. All shall be well in the end. You will see it for yourself one day, Jesus promised her.[19]

The question we may ask ourselves is: what do I see when considering my world? Not superficially, but at a deeper level. In special education we are always busy in figuring out what might be going through the minds of our pupils. How they perceive what is happening to them in life. But we may be slow in putting that question to ourselves. It tends to pass us by. An answer is hard to find. Perhaps because our faith comes up short when confronted with life's complexities. We fail to answer the ultimate question adequately. What, really, truly and undeniably, do I believe, and why? Deciding on that is a struggle. Let me give you a way forward that has helped me, derived from Lady Julian's insights. Perhaps you will find it useful.

The cell she lived in for three decades has three narrow windows. One looks into the church against which the small room has been built. It gives a view of the altar. Julian of Norwich could participate in the mass and receive the Eucharist each Sunday. Also, she could contemplate God at any time with the altar in sight.

The second was a window for practical matters such as food and cleanliness. Lady Julian had a cook and a maid serving her. The third window had a cloth over it preventing the anchoress from being seen. It was for people from outside to approach and ask their questions. There would have been a door as well, leading into a small walled garden. Into that setting Julian of Norwich was anchored down until her departure into heaven.

Figuratively, in my life, I apply these windows as follows. The first one allows me to come close to God. The second concerns the help I receive from God by the Holy Spirit. The third window is my interaction with the world, the perceptions I hold regarding it. In all of that, I am guided by Scripture and Lady Julian's revelations. And I need to keep in mind that every window is a window of love.

When I look through the first window at God, what do I perceive? Julian of Norwich's primary understanding is that God is love! God cannot but love. All God's acts are those of love and goodness. Divine goodness fills all his creatures and all God's works completely and does forever overflow in them.[20] To us it will not ever seem that way because of all the suffering around. How can a loving God allow that to happen? Before considering that vexing question, I would like to focus on myself for a moment. If I leave the perplexities of life aside, and just look at God, how does the reality of his love impact me? How, if doing likewise, might it affect you? That partly depends on your idea about God and about yourself as a person. Lady Julian suggests that in getting to know God, you will begin to better understand your own person. Your faith will reveal your true self.[21] To a measure that is. For your real self is so deeply grounded in God, that it is easier to know God than to know yourself.[22] That is what Julian of Norwich understood. God knows, that you are far from perfect and yet God is completely enamoured with you.[23] The question is: can you believe that? If you find that difficult, just tell yourself often that in God's eyes you're okay. Or, in other words, learn to love yourself with your eyes wide open. There is no need for perfection. Just seeking to do right as best as possible, is all that is required.

Self-perception is never flawless, Julian explained. She paused for a moment and recollected her thoughts.

Continual exposure to life gives us perspectives that usually are little more than a point of view, also about ourselves. That view will be partly right, but it cannot ever be fully correct. Before God our distorted self-assessment is completely immaterial. God loves us unconditionally. And we are freely invited to accept that - that we deserve that marvellous love. By all means throw up all kinds of qualifications. In the end those matter not one bit. God declares you loveable and would like your spirit to rest in that reality. That is what Julian of Norwich saw.

Julian let that information sink in and continued.

Through the second window in my story, the serving one, the anchoress was ministered to in her daily needs. It asks the question, how does God care for each of us? As mentioned, it is God's wish that we know God and that we know ourselves. And we must humbly accept that our true self, the good person we essentially are, is opposed by sin and weakness.[24] This awareness is not at the forefront of our minds normally. We tend not to see our vulnerabilities very clearly, Julian of Norwich suggests. Lovingly the Holy Spirit is continually active in reducing that blindness.[25] Not to accuse us, but to open our eyes to the true reality of what we are facing. In her book she makes an interesting observation about the Lord's attitude towards we having to live under the influences of sin. I will read it out to you.

For love never allows him to be without pity; and when we fall into sin, and neglect recollection of him and the protection of our own soul, then Christ bears all alone the burden of us. And so he remains, moaning and groaning.[26]

When we fail, turn away from him, the Lord hurts. But he makes sure that our soul remains protected in his love. Not ever is he not involved with us and that at a very personal level. The Lord ministers his grace continually. He will never leave us to ourselves and will always protect us from blame in his sight.[27] Jesus is our Helper, who does not point a finger, but understands our struggles. And of course, far from everything that happens to us is because of personal failings.[28] Jesus knows that, hurts with us, and bears our burdens in loving care. We need to honour him with reciprocating love. Troubles will come, hard times appear, but as we trust in his love and close presence we will make it through. The Lord told Lady Julian strongly that we will not be overcome.[29] This second window, which supplies our daily needs, is the one of God's love and care. I look through that window often, Julian told the staff – by faith. It brings the right perspective into my circumstances.

Time was moving on. Much more could be said, but not this morning. Julian ended by explaining the last window.

The third window was the one through which Julian of Norwich gave counsel. People came to seek her wisdom. It must have been based on how she viewed God's involvement with our world. God had not deserted it, of that the anchoress was convinced. The world is essentially good, but marred by sin.[30] If we can look past the suffering, and that does not mean ignoring it, we must believe the hand of God to be at work in a creation that has fallen, but that has remained in God. God's goodness has not departed from the creation. Rather, he guards it attentively. That raises the question of suffering and its origin: the power of sin. Julian of Norwich understood that sin is alien to God, completely unrelated to love. She could never see sin is her visions and believed, in her own words, that "it has no kind of substance, no share in being, nor can it be recognised except by the pain caused by it."[31] When she asked Jesus why sin exists, he replied with just three words. "Sin is necessary."[32] She was told not to pursue this; instead to focus on him and his love for her. On what he had accomplished. She understood that God is working out a final outcome, a new creation. Its glory would have been impossible without Jesus entering our present sinful stage and gaining a victory over it.[33] Furthermore, without our temporary pains here on earth, the exalted knowledge of God which we shall have one day in heaven, could never be ours to receive.[34] Julian of Norwich saw that we shall understand that when with Christ's in heaven and agree that yes: God's plan is perfect regardless of our current troubles[35]. You may find that hard to believe. Almost too glib to be true. However, your assessment in no way makes the insight invalid. In fact, it would be difficult to come up with an idea that answers questions about the struggles of our world better. And it must be remembered, that Julian of Norwich received this understanding from her visions. This insight was not an intellectually constructed answer to placate a suffering world.

She had wondered about the non-Christians, the pagans, who according to church teaching are destined to hell. Jesus had insisted that all would be well. How could that be, if people were to get so lost? She had asked the Lord about it and gained no answer beyond the assurance that: 'What is impossible to you is not impossible to me. I shall make everything well.'[36] From this she concluded that she should not dismiss the teachings of the church where those differed from her visions. Rather, remain faithful to the faith as presented and trust in the great deed that one day God will do to make all things well indeed. In other words, let it be.[37]

So, how do I look at the world? Julian concluded her presentation with that question. We have to maintain our hope in a God who cares about everyone and everything deeply and who is in the process of making everything well in the end. In the meantime, let us step as lightly[38] as we are able to. We must live life to the full and try to carry our burdens without too heavy a heart. That may be very difficult at times and don't blame yourself when it seems impossible. Just know that God is near. God understands. God hurts with us. In everything seek to keep an open eye on the three windows of love. Keep an eye on Julian's windows. Personally, they give me comfort and hopefully will do likewise for you.

With that suggestion Julian ended her talk. Applause followed as expected. It seemed genuine.

A few of staff expressed their appreciation during the midmorning break. Julian felt a bit deflated. It was normal someone once had told her, when communicating to a group with intent.

9

NUTTY WAS RUNNING FREELY through the cow paddocks checking out fence posts, trees and whatever took her fancy. Nick had taken a long walk in the green countryside not because the dog was in need of it, Nutty ran about plenty, but because he himself felt the urge to get away from the house. Clear his head with fresh air. Spending time in the open was therapeutic and a frequent exercise. Down a slope they were approaching Nick's favourite spot. Where the creek that ran through his property featured a mini rapid with water audibly speeding over smooth stones. He loved that sound and the log on the edge to sit on. It allowed for a great view down a dale. Unless a fog enveloped the undulating land. Even that would charm the eye. Today, all was clear and deep shades from a bright sun dappled the landscape.

Nick let the surroundings penetrate his soul. Slowly he sat down on the log. The water gurgled, the birds sang and the breeze made its own particular sound. Of late a new awareness had begun to present itself during these reflective moments in nature. Since a young age, Nick had been sensitive to atmosphere. When entering a room it was the first impression that would come his way. What the place felt like. He had begun to perceive things differently lately, sitting on this thick log. Likewise during his walks when giving the environment the attention it deserved. It offered a clarity unlike before, as if he could look deeper into its reality. This sensitivity, however subtle, could not simply be explained as a function of imagination. The impressions were intuitive and happened unannounced. They were a communication of some sort. Nick took pleasure from it. As a musician, he detected the different moods of sound in nature depending on the weather. Today, with the sun out and only little breeze, the sound had the colour of orange.

A certain reason for this newly found ability would be his diminishing introspection caused by grief. Nick was sure of it. He felt a little better these days. The other was his exposure to the jazz music borrowed from Tom. All his life Nick had lived with the sounds of the city never realising how much these had influenced his identity as a musician. Or a person for that matter. The energy of city bustle was addictive, as if carried by a dynamic that drove you on almost in spite of yourself. Slowing down would get you out of synch with the rhythm of your environment and was subliminally avoided. Even taking the occasional breather, which of course you should do, was a breather with the city at its foundation. For Nick it had been a good life, one he had liked. His music fitted the nature of modernity and reflected bare concrete, harsh light and the cut and thrust of making do. Metal and its high decibel projection spoke of a place that never slept and that interfered with consciousness. The primitive driving force of drum and bass hooked into the deep-seated urges dormant within every person. Nick had always enjoyed Melbourne and his music. When he lost Helen all that changed.

Ever since this loss, the force of city life had likewise become lost to him. He had not been up to it, those energy levels. Nor had he been interested anymore. Country life seemed the better option. Nick was still well capable of metal, but in a different way. Pumping out aggressive bass lines that gelled with his anger had indeed offered a release of deeply felt frustration. It happened soon after moving into the old dairy. Once he felt ready to take up the guitar again. The futility of these outbursts had dawned on him quickly. For how long could he keep expressing this kind of aggressive music, and that while on his own? Clearly, it was a dead end street. As a sound, the bass could connect with grief rather well. But belting the life out of four or five fat strings willy-nilly was dumb. Good music required subtlety.

Sitting on his log Nick noticed a bird hidden amongst the foliage of an elm tree singing brightly. The freedom of birdsong reminded of the jazz music Tom had given him to take home, Nick mused. The selection involved popular artists known also beyond the world of jazz. But for one trio. He had mentioned two of the artists during his discussion with Tom.

From the moment the first trumpet notes of Miles Davis' *Kind of Blue* bounced off the walls of his kitchen, jazz became his new interest. With John Coltrane on the saxophone the tune was a fabulous effort in sound and improvisation. Nick had heard it before, years ago. But being engrossed in the building of a repertoire for their metal band, he had given it little attention. Now *Kind of Blue* made him crash into his easy chair with Nutty soon following suit on her blanket nearby. A glass of whiskey to stroke his melancholic mood and he drifted off into the blue yonder. Alternating between discerning the bass lines and feeling his hurt. The music seemed to take the sharp edge off his pain. That pain remained real enough, but felt more manageable. Around midnight, a sharp cold had woken him from a deep slumber.

From Tom's book he learned that the roots of jazz were in blues and ragtime. He discovered the developments in jazz over time. There were few limits in creating soundscapes. It aimed at spontaneously connecting head and heart, though this spontaneity could be an illusion. Whatever the truth of that, modern jazz was never highly scripted, leaving space for musical interpretation. Nick fell in love with it. Already the next day, after *Kind of Blue*, he had grabbed his bass and softly superimposed his own arrangements. *Miles in the Sky*, being more rock than jazz, was the obvious start in doing so. It aligned with his own musical background. Nick enjoyed the unique rhythm of Dave Brubeck's *Take Five* and found Astrud Gilberto's voice singing A *Girl from Ipanema* enchanting. Not to forget the partnership between guitarist Joao Gilberto, Astrud's husband, and Stan Getz on tenor sax. Nick was grateful for his good fortune in meeting Vorque. Providence was a better word, no doubt, but he preferred not to dwell on that thought. His communications with God remained fragile. Not even the vibraphone of the Modern Jazz Quartet, which lightened his mood with glimmers of hope, would change that. Jazz with its wide vistas of sound and beauty opened up a new world. A world he was growing into. The meaning of sound became much enlarged to him, including the sounds he found in nature. He enjoyed being out amongst the fields and trees now like never before.

With the sun lowering in the sky he proceeded towards home weaving amongst Charles' grazing black cattle. Nick avoided too close a contact with the young calves. No need to stir up a large mother's attention. Nutty had learned to leave the animals well alone unless she was instructed otherwise. She was running way ahead, quite unconcerned about her boss, who surely would follow. Nick saw no need to whistle his best friend back. The more she ran, the quieter she would be once settling down for the evening. There was no fear that Nutty would be silly enough to enrage a snake either. Those too, she would leave well alone, though barking in anger. Unless they intruded into his yard close to the house, Nick wasn't bothered about snakes. You just needed to keep your eyes well open. They were hard to detect even when openly basking in the sun. Snakes would only become aggressive when threatened. They preferred to slither away from people.

Coming through at the back of the old dairy Nick pulled a few potatoes out of his vegetable garden, also some carrots. He enjoyed growing things and had planted a number of bushes round about to give his place more character. It is all in the soil preparation an experienced gardener had told him, and in selecting suitable plants. Loosening up the soil and adding a dose of potting mix with fertilizer seemed to have done the trick. The bushes were taking well.

The potatoes and carrots were washed under the tap outside. The green foliage cut off to be thrown onto the compost heap. Nick intended to make a shepherd's pie. After slicing up the carrots and an onion, plus a glove of fresh garlic, he steamed those above the boiling potatoes. Quality beef mince, nicely spiced, was fried well through and placed in the bottom of a ceramic dish, mixed with pasta sauce for further taste and moisture. The steamed vegetables were spread out on top of the meat followed by potatoes mashed with milk and two raw eggs. Nick added a layer of shredded cheese and the dish disappeared into the Aga for reheating and browning. It would be dinner for a few days.

After dinner, washing his plate and cutlery – the mess made in preparing the meal having been cleared earlier – Nick decided to play the only CD he had as yet not listened to. The piece was an hour long without a break, thus the reason for the delay. Tonight Nick felt he was up to it. A trio from Sydney called The Necks played a composition entitled *Drive By*. Monotonous and repetitive, with the musical dynamics changing between spacious ethereal sounds and some harder hitting moments, it represented modern life, including the idea of a helicopter produced by the synthesizer. The music reminded him of a non-stop stream of traffic, which the title was referring to. There were no obvious chord changes. The drum and bass for minutes on end played the same few notes and rhythms, with subtle changes as the music was progressing. The occasional piano notes floated over the melodic bass of the keyboard. To Nick's ear the music was layered in two levels, the rhythm section and the tonal. Not ever was there a melody involved. The piano, playing single notes and so few that a gifted child might accomplish it, brought one of Helen's favourite classical composers to mind: Arvo Paert. Gradually, Nick felt himself sucked in by the music. That was how he would think of it. It happened quite slowly with the mesmerizing monotony of drum and bass beginning to work deeply into his senses. Just driving on at base level. It summed up his life at present. He took no effort to connect with the tonal levels of the music. The piano floated in his consciousness without meaning.

For no noticeable reason, that suddenly changed. To Nick's surprise, the tonal began to present itself as his pain. A confrontation that momentarily took his breath away. He was staring his pain in the face - and in doing so the reason for it. He realised that the pain would never fully cease. It would dim over time, which lately he had begun to notice. The question raised during this encounter, almost as if from person to person, was simple: For how long will you fight me? It was communicated without aggression and seemed almost sympathetic. Nick didn't know how to answer that question. He felt just to let it be; not give it any thought right now. As the music moved on, Nick drifted along with it, unaware of his surroundings. He had closed his eyes long ago. Suddenly he was taken by a new sensation, kind of strange. It happened while the piano sound, which Nick now identified as pain in his experience, played a beautiful little progression. Pain and beauty – that made no sense. Then he began to sense a force behind the pain. It was far more dominant and worthy of being called beautiful. He understood it to be the power of love. It hovered in the background with complete authority and seemed to validate the existence of his cutting pain in an indescribable manner. Nick would never be able to put that impression into words. Even though it was very distinct. The experience fizzled out in harmony with how The Necks ended *Drive By*. The music becoming simpler, more relaxed and slowly disappearing. Open-ended, as if the statement made would prevail quite apart from and beyond its presentation. In the resulting silence Nick opened his eyes.

The next morning, over a cup of strong coffee, Nick made a decision. He would see himself as a victim of his circumstances no longer. Pain and grief were the stuff of life. Better not to fight it. He should take it on board without feeling sorry for himself, if that were manageable. It was as far as he got in response to the strange musical experience of the previous night. Perhaps one day he might understand it more. One impression it left was clear. Better to have loved and got hurt, than not having loved at all. On his way out into the yard he looked at Helen's picture hanging unobtrusively on the kitchen wall. Silently he said, thank you, with tears beginning to well up in his eyes. He would make a good day of it.

10

'LET'S PLAY BLUE,' Aluka suggested. She was seated behind the baby grand and began to play the piano keys with a light touch creating a melancholic sound while the others prepared their instruments. Nick had arrived at the beautiful home to be greeted by Tom, his wife and Jeremy, a drummer. Soon after the introductions, they had moved to the music corner of the big room. Just a jam session, Tom had explained. Aluka would start off with a simple progression. Jeremy was to play a suitable rhythm, which Nick would support on the bass. Tom himself planned to drift in and out on the guitar as he saw fit. It would enable him to listen how piano, bass and drum gelled, Nick concluded.

Fine music began to fill the room. Obviously, Aluka knew how to play in blue using jazz chords overlaid with a thin tonal composition. She moved from minor to major 7 and back within a few bars. Jeremy soon found the correct feel on the drums and for Nick all was cool. He understood this music, knew what Aluka was doing, and flowed in with an ease that quite surprised him.

Good musicians recognise soundscapes as a language. If you can communicate in it, all is well. The development of his skills in playing jazz these last few weeks was paying off, Nick discovered. Tom picked up his guitar only near the end and for most of the time sat listening with a smile on his face. Once he did join in, the music lifted another notch. The guitar gracefully harmonising with the piano, never dominant and never timid. Almost reluctantly the piece was brought to an end.

They took a breather with hardly a word being spoken. Music could have that effect on a person. While fiddling her fingers over the black and white keys without intent, Aluka suggested they might play in red next. She began an intro with her hands losing the soft touch on the keys. Still playing jazz, but in the way of rock. Like *Myles in the Sky*, Nick thought. It took a little while to perceive how she was moving along with her chords, the flow being more complicated than was usual for rock music. But soon Nick's preferred lines on the bass were decided on. Once sorted, all came naturally. Tom cut in from the start. In closing, Aluka played solely rock without a single jazz chord, just for fun. Jeremy surely knew how to drum it and was careful not to overpower the others. Musicians needed to be mindful of that. The sound bounced off the large windows with a vengeance. Five beats on snare and cymbals, in the manner that rock music might end when unscripted, finished the session. It was time for a break. Coffee and small-talk. Tom took effort to set Nick at ease, the stranger amongst the four with Jeremy being a house guest. The aggression he was known for as Vorque was completely lacking. It simply had been a stage persona, Nick figured.

Their next piece was *The Girl from Ipanema.*

'Tom will play sax on the guitar,' Aluka teased her husband with a smile.

He could never make that happen, but played worthy of Joao Gilberto. Once Aluka began to sing, Nick's heart missed a beat. This lady was seriously talented. Cheekily she gave him a wink to show that she had noticed his surprise. Embarrassed, Nick quickly looked away. The piece was his most relaxed effort of the day for he knew it well. Aluka extended the usual length of the song. It was fun to play.

With the last notes of *Ipanema* drifting away, Tom initiated a discussion about the potential fusion of jazz and metal. Might it be possible? It is like playing in black, he suggested. Jeremy doubted that he could play both styles sort of simultaneously. The best might be to alternate between the two. Still he would give mixing it up a try. Nick saw possibilities, but could not be that certain, never having tried it out. Tom explained that with Aluka he had worked on jazz/metal already. But without the support of a rhythm section he could not be sure of its success. All he wished to find out today was whether the style could be developed over time. Just for his personal interest. They would give it a go.

Tom began to play a riff with a hard hitting sound that carried a distinct jazz flavour. Jeremy gave it a metal beat for a while, which slowly became less forceful but kept its penetration. They worked at it for some minutes. Nick busied himself with designing an approach for the bass in his mind. He was accomplished enough to play that without fail once called upon. When Tom gave the nod, the bass slotted in smoothly. Nick tried not to fall back on metal overly much, which would have been easy, but to concentrate on the jazz. He needed to get a feel out of his strings that somehow was able to blend the two genres. When she considered the men to have reached their best, Aluka joined in. She added the layer missing from the overall sound, the piano being ideally suited to creating and supporting jazz. The jazz/metal idea seemed to be working.

Nick really enjoyed himself. If only the experience didn't have to be so brief. At best, he might expect this kind of fun sporadically, if he were that lucky. Tom seemed to spend much of his time in Melbourne and perhaps around the world. Coming to Merton to play jazz/metal would not happen often.

They repeated the jazz/metal exercise with another of Tom's compositions, after which he thanked them for their efforts. He was much the wiser now. It was time for lunch.

Jeremy and Nick were asked whether they would like a Coopers Pale. Tom suggested they take a seat at the table on the decking outside. He would get some food ready in the kitchen with Aluka's help. With beer in hand the two men made their way through the enormous glass sliding doors. Once seated, neither of them spoke, at first.

'Where you from, Nick?' Jeremy asked eventually.

'Melbourne.'

Nick returned the question.

'I'm from Sydney,' Jeremy explained.

He sounded completely Australian, Nick thought. Though Jeremy was an Asian person. There were many Asian immigrants in Australia, the number increasing by the year.

'Born there,' Jeremy said, guessing Nick's reaction. 'The name is Chen.'

Nick mentioned his own surname, it being Avero.

Before lunch arrived he learned that Jeremy was known in the music industry as Mr Chen and from an early age had been interested in jazz. However, his first serious stint as a musician had been with a rock band. Just like Charlie Watts of The Stones, Nick thought. That comment he kept to himself. Jeremy had discovered his dislike of touring, being away from home too often. Also, he could never be certain of earning enough to support a family. His wife desired children and for her to stop working once they arrived. Fully subscribing to that sentiment he had decided to develop his IT skills further. Presently, Jeremy owned a small company that was doing well. There was now time again for his other love besides his family – jazz music.

Nick perceived him to be a complete person – capable at whatever he decided on and making no big deal of it. Relaxed they sat together enjoying the view. In turn Nick explained his own circumstances. Jeremy, who in age surpassed him by some years, accepted the information without comment. When asked what band Nick had played in he seemed to know of it and made appreciative comments. Though in IT, he had not lost contact with the Australian music scene, Nick discovered.

Lunch was served - a large platter with all sorts of goodies supported by a choice of fine wines. Tom asked Nick how he was getting on with improving the old dairy. Aluka wished to know what had attracted him to it. Also, she had noticed a brown kelpie running around and wondered whether Nick might introduce her before leaving. It would be his pleasure. The conversation was as if between friends. Having eaten at a leisurely pace, Tom asked Jeremy to follow him to the dining table in the main room. He wished to ask a few questions.

'Tom has some money invested in IT,' Aluka explained, seeking to justify the separation.

Nick had no problem with that and was happy to remain with his hostess. She was an attractive person. Obviously, partly of African descent and kind of regal looking. He would not probe into her background.

'You understand my music, Nick' Aluka told him. 'You are also very talented.'

Nick was aware of his considerable musical ability. But few folk had ever mentioned it apart from Helen. Good bands took it for granted.

'Thank you,' he replied.

'Tom told me about your wife. I'm sorry.'

Nick nodded, unwilling to respond. Now was not the time to discuss Helen.

'That's why you understand my music, I guess.'

This remark needed some thought. But before he could respond, Aluka explained.

'Jazz, originally, was both a happy music in party town New Orleans as well as deeply blue in response to circumstances that often for many were not encouraging. It's the known African gift to laugh happily amongst friends while facing many challenges. My dad told me about that, based on his time in South Africa.'

'You're from South Africa,' Nick enquired. It made sense.

'No, I was born in Melbourne. My mother was South African.'

Nick noticed that Aluka spoke of her mother in the past tense.

'Was?' he asked.

'Yes. It's a sad story. Sad for me in losing my mum at seventeen, but particularly for my father.'

'What happened?'

'My dad is German. As a young man he emigrated to South Africa. To cut a long story short, he fell madly in love with my mother, who was black. In the sixties, with apartheid still firmly entrenched, that was anathema. He left for Australia with the South African police sort of on his heels. They turned a blind eye because he was leaving their country. It was a problem neatly solved. He thought, he had lost my mum forever, but managed to get her out to here, eventually. They were so very happy. Then cancer struck.'

Nick said nothing and immediately thought of Helen. He felt completely inadequate.

'What I mean is,' Aluka explained, 'you cannot play like you do, nor can I, unless you are acquainted with sorrow.' She looked out over the fields for a moment. 'That's what I believe. We're kindred spirits, Nick. And it shows in our music.'

Nick felt a little pleased at this observation. He didn't know what to say and steered the conversation elsewhere.

'You are classically trained,' he ventured.

Aluka smiled. 'Very perceptive, Nick.' She took a sip of her wine. He couldn't help but like her.

'It was my mother's wish. She and dad were always busy with Bach and the like. I had piano lessons from an early age. The classical training was actually very helpful, though it will never be my future.'

'And then you met Tom.'

Nick took a risk with that question which might be considered inquisitive. Aluka seemed not to mind.

'Yes, in Germany. I was staying there with relatives in Berlin, doing a little studio work, mostly backup singing. One day, busy at the studio, the producer was throwing a party that evening. He thought I might as well stay on, join the fun. I felt like hiding in a corner, literally did, knowing none of the people present.'

'But Tom sought you out and said you were the most interesting person in the room,' Nick guessed.

'Yes.' Aluke seemed surprised. Then faintly smiled. 'That happened to you, did it?' she wondered.

Nick confirmed that it had, in Merton, at the local pub.

'Tom is such a nice man, you know. Denim and lace. He grew up the hard way in a struggling family. He is tough and smart, and kind at heart.'

They stopped talking for a while.

'Listen, Nick,' Aluka continued without preamble. 'Tom wants to start a jazz/metal band called *M-Jazz Indigo*. Are you interested in joining? I told him that you would be a perfect fit.'

Nick was completely lost for words. He had never imagined that Tom was planning another band. He just looked at Aluka.

'I'll take that as a yes then,' she concluded, grinning. 'It will be a pleasure, Nick.'

The plans were explained to the future bass player of *M-Jazz Indigo* without him uttering any sensible word in response, still working through his surprise.

'Don't forget, I'd like to meet your dog before you go,' Aluka reminded him and began to clear the table.

Half an hour later Nutty was chasing a tennis ball Aluka had conjured up. Jeremy expressed his pleasure at them meeting up again soon. Tom warmly thanked Nick for the day. You're good, mate, he said.

Back at home, Nick saw Julian's famous statement hanging unobtrusively on his kitchen wall: *Alle Shalle Be Wele*. He also remembered Helen's last words to him. Oh Nick, don't have me worry about you, hey? He missed her very much and felt his loss acutely.

11

ONCE A WEEK, Sister Julian served in a soup kitchen. Today her mind was not on the job as usual. She had made sure to put on her golden necklace with a little cross. The one she was fond of but never wore to school for the children would soon get hold of it. She knew all the regulars coming for a meal and was determined to be friendly. This evening the dish was a curry, plus salad and bread. It was a nourishing and balanced food. Dessert was jelly and cream. Upon receiving his plate Gordon said his usual hellos and when asked briefly how things were going answered just with the simple word 'yeah.' It was his stock answer to any interest shown in his wellbeing and could mean anything. Trudy began to relate whatever took her interest that moment, holding up the line of takers. Julian tactfully moved her on. Some of the guests she had not seen before. There were always newcomers most of them drifting through to other places. Serving the destitute of society gave her pleasure, but today she noticed it less.

There were so many facets to human experience, like a

diamond with many small flat sections. All illuminated by an inner sparkle however dull and grubby some sections might be. Every person has a spark in the soul, placed there by God, German mystic Meister Eckhart had held. Julian of Norwich had understood that every soul when coming into existence is united to the Creator, who would not allow a double death, but sent his Son to prevent that.[39] It aligned with Scripture that revealed all to exist and hold together in Christ even though in a fallen state.[40] Instead of facing a second death and thus becoming fully alienated from God, creation would be re-birthed.

So many facets of experience, Julian reflected, and who is to judge? She thought of Celia sitting in the sand, filling her fists with the gritty golden stuff and letting it sift through her fingers close up to her eyes, over and over again. But each time seemed to be necessary for Celia, like she was imprinting some wonder on her brain. The passage of time was unknown to her. The moment was now, always now. Might that be why it was so difficult to transition her to the next activity? Would shifting the moment cause consternation? Celia, she was one facet of the diamond, and just as worthy as the next. She carried the same internal spark as all the other facets. Why should there only be one template for being a person. How fascinating it was that a minute alteration in chromosomes could produce such unique people, who added to the beauty of the diamond.

Julian carried one of the large empty pans to the kitchen. There had been enough food today with little left. Oversupply raised the question of dumping, which was avoided as much as possible. A shortage of meals would start a scurrying about in the kitchen to produce extra. That had its problems. Soon it would be time for washing up. The plates would be near empty for many guests were fast eaters. Not like Melanie, Julian thought, a child so tiny and fragile even though she was twelve. Her body could not grow with the sparse nourishment she was able to digest. It took ages for her to finish her meal, but she knew what she liked and how much of it. It was important to respect her choices. She needed to be given time and space to make her own decisions. Melanie was another facet of the diamond.

Julian had trouble being alert while serving because of an experience earlier that day. It had been unexpected.

Father Ivan had officiates Mass this morning at school, a once a term event, to which parents were invited. Thomas high-jacked proceedings by wandering through the gym at the start. Noticing the holy bread he began to eat. Father Ivan went with the flow for he understood the situation. It had been a moment of beauty for Julian. An intellectually disabled child partaking of the host because it looked good to eat. Jesus would be smiling.

Thomas was helped to take his place amongst the other children. They tried to follow their song sheets, rode with the currents as they interpreted them, and responded honestly according to their ability. Always, their reactions were varied and concentration levels non-existent with most of them. There was hyperactivity, incomprehension, glazed glances and withdrawal. Those children who never took a step back in the classroom were not inclined to do so during the mass. Strong projections of personality were noticeable. I see something you don't see, feel something you can't, and hear something that escapes you. The kind of behaviour that is normal in a special school.

Father Ivan was a good priest, very empathetic and embracing. He had followed convention in distributing the wine and bread but never mentioned that you needed to be a Catholic to partake. Either, he took it for granted that people were aware of it, or had his reasons. Parents, whom Julian knew to be Catholic, received the host. As did a few non-Catholic Christian staff members. Julian saw no problems with that. In the larger churches it was often unknown whether all of those taking bread and wine were actually of the Catholic faith. Christ would receive anyone. Still, if the church had decided to be particular about participation that was fine. Adults could make up their minds. If Catholicism appealed to them, then learn the catechism and become confirmed.

A number of children at Talitha Cumi, who had been confirmed, were offered the host also. Others received a blessing. Disabled children of Catholic families who had reached the age of confirmation, but would never be able to understand the catechism, might receive the sacrament all the same. This permission was gained through the local parish in acknowledgement of the difficulties presented in the wine and bread becoming the actual mystical body of Christ. Transubstantiation, as it was called, is a pivotal doctrine to Catholic belief. Children with an intellectual disability might not be able to understand that as the consecrated host the bread and wine no longer are ordinary, of the kind found at home, but extra-ordinary. This should not become a barrier to participation, the church had decided. Jesus loved his disabled friends dearly, had deposited his own spark in their hearts, and they should be welcome at the altar with full rights, Julian believed. She was aware that dioceses might differ in their approach regarding the sacraments and disability. It could become quite unjust with parents hurting. Fortunately, that was not so at Talitha Cumi.

Julian had observed how the mothers and their children came to Father Ivan. A number of the older children had eaten the wafer and drunk some wine. They were attentively assisted. Others obtained a blessing. The sight of a mother and child that showed noticeable care and love between them had suddenly stung Julian's heart. Again she faced up to the fact that though adoring them, as a Sister she would never have a child of her own. For a moment she had closed her eyes in consternation, the feeling of loss being so real. It had taken her breath away. The word sacrifice had come to mind. But without carrying the usual conviction that it had to be that way. What was happening to her? What should she make of it? She wiped the meal tables in the soup kitchen vigorously and thought about the renewing of her vows.

Getting home late to her room Julian knew that falling asleep would be a problem. Though she was tired from a busy day. Praying would be difficult too for she had a head churning with questions, and one in particular. She was experienced enough spiritually to know that discernment took time. On the other hand, when sensing a prompting it needed following up on. This evening it seemed that she should not immediately drop the question of motherhood. She should begin to work towards an answer. The issue had been building over the last few months and she had ignored it. She opened the book containing the long version of Lady Julian's visions at the motherhood of God. It was the only text she knew that dealt with the topic of motherhood from the perspective of revelation rather than culture. Motherhood was not a concept exclusive to the created realm.

Understanding Julian of Norwich needed precise reading and reflection. The mystic seemed to circle around her perceptions of what she had seen, interwove them, and in giving comment could take a variety of perspectives. Ideas could be multi-layered, her presentation medieval in style. But her thoughts were never incoherent. Julian had studied the chapters on motherhood[41] before and now had decided on what she considered to be the central theme. Her interpretation, though simple and at times taking license with regard to the wording, did the text justice, she believed.

Everything happened because of God's love – God cannot but love and all God's works are works of love. Motherhood in God is a dynamic similar to birthing – a creative act that brings newness into being. Fatherhood in God is the initial thought without which this action cannot happen. We are a twinkle in the Father's eye, so to speak. The initial thought with God concerns us being spiritually created. This is the first stage of our being and the most important one. Julian of Norwich called that our *substantial* nature or high substance. It corresponds with the spark in our soul mentioned by Meister Eckhart. In the process of us being birthed as a person, a birthing that happens *in* Christ, our *sensual* nature, the lower part of our substance, comes about. It completes what it means to be human. Both the higher and the lower find pre-eminence in Christ, the Second Person in the Trinity, in whom the birthing of all of creation takes place. Furthermore, the creative thoughts in the Father's mind are those of the Son. The Holy Spirit is the divine Person in whom creation becomes endowed with grace. This understanding shows God to be a Father, taking the initiative, as well as being a Mother, producing the creative act – giving birth. The Holy Spirit ensures that all is cared for. As all of creation originates with the Father and finds existence in the Son, it is warranted to call Jesus our Mother.

Julian had always found this understanding interesting and helpful. She herself had come to the conclusion that there was no sexuality in God. Even though human perception because of existential circumstances might assign it. To her surprise she had found support in that from Julian of Norwich[42]. Humanly speaking, God the Father refers to the One in whom the initial seed-thought originates which then comes about in the Son. This original seed-thought in the Father co-exists in the Son and the creative act of birthing eventuates in the Son. Without the seed there cannot be a birthing. On earth, without a male, a female cannot conceive. Lady Julian held that our higher substance, our substantial nature, is spiritual and exists in God before we are created as an earthly being. The seed-thought in the Father and the Son becomes an earthly reality in Jesus our Mother. The idea of Jesus our Mother was not exclusive to Julian of Norwich but uncommon.

Julian reflected further. Her own thoughts based on what she had read previously. Perhaps God was presented to us as male because in a sense God was a seed carrier. Also, Jesus had a Father in heaven for on earth Mary was his mother. It was how divinity and humanity had united. Sexuality was not actually an issue here beyond the seed being accepted by the womb. Nor will it be in heaven for there is no giving in marriage and procreation in that eternal abode.[43] God as Father, fully a male image, was a troublesome thought. It excluded the female principle from the godhead. Mother Jesus, equally important, set the balance right. God fully understood motherhood and might be approached accordingly.

Julian liked that idea very much. She was skimming through some of the pages of *Julian's Revelations* but could not muster enough concentration. An intellectual answer to her problem was not what she needed. The anchoress had been a mother, had lost a child it was believed, and had written a few words about what being a mother meant without turning it into theology. In describing Christ's motherhood though, she extolled the role of the earthly mother. Julian found the sentences she was looking for.

> The kind, loving mother who knows and sees the need of her child guards it very tenderly, as the nature and condition of motherhood will have. And always as the child grows in age and in stature, she act differently, but she does not change her love.[44]

It was oil on the fire of Julian's feelings; a mother loving a child. It played within her as a dull ache. The issue had been smouldering subconsciously for a while and could be ignored no longer. She asked the Lord to give her peace and imagined him to be unperturbed. All shall be well, were the words that came to mind. Comforting - but so completely open-ended.

A week later Julian was invited to a teacher friend's home for the birthday celebrations of her one year old son. Her friend was so happy with her child. While walking home Julian decided to discuss the renewing of her vows with the community leader. Ask for a holiday to visit family. Being away from religious life for a few weeks might give her clarity. Perhaps it would be the circuit breaker in her dilemma. A definitive answer was needed at thirty-three years of age.

PART TWO

12

LATE AFTERNOON on a rainy day Nick drove into the yard of Charles' farm with Nutty next to him. The rain was coming down too heavily for the dog to travel in the tray and catch pneumonia. She was fogging up the windscreen with her breath. Nick drove carefully peering through a patch of glass that offered the best view. Nutty recognised where they were headed and was excited. She was a ray of sunshine to Nick. He had no idea what life would have been like without his dog. Had no intention thinking about it. Fortunately, his future looked better than the recent past. In the music industry nothing was ever a certainty though.

Wherever Nick went, Nutty followed – a loyal and good companion. Soon however he would have to go places where the presence of a dog was unwelcome. The thought grated on him, but it had to be. Nick felt he had a solution and that it would not be a problem.

The kitchen door of the farmhouse opened before he could knock. The approach of his car would have been noticed. When living on the land noises besides those from animals and birds are few. Usually quietness reigns unless the farmers are busy with their machinery. It would be unusual at the end of a working day. Nick was expecting Charles to be at home. It was Mandy though who appeared in the doorway. When Nutty was about to jump up toward her she quickly and gently kept the kelpie down ruffling the dog's head. Muddy paws on her jeans Mandy could do without.

'Come in, Nick,' she said kindly. Mandy liked her neighbour, who had been living close by for over a year.

Nick told Nutty to settle on the covered veranda and stepped into the warm kitchen. He noticed the table was set for dinner. It was early for an evening meal and he apologised for interrupting so close to dinnertime. It had not been his intention.

'Charles has a meeting in Mansfield soon,' Mandy explained with a smile. 'He's in the yard checking out on a calf. He shouldn't be long.'

Nick felt a little uncomfortable all the same and it seemed to show.

'Don't worry about it, Nick. You're always welcome. How about I add a plate and you can join us?'

Mandy did not look what many people expected of a farmer's wife. She liked her clothes, was educated and didn't show her age. It would be nearing fifty. She was a hard worker, Nick imagined. At a farm there was always much to do. Many a meal would be prepared fresh from scratch, rather than out of tins and plastic packaging.

Mandy looked at this attractive and sensitive man with his ponytail and took charge in deciding about his meal. 'That's settled then,' she concluded and walked to the sideboard.

While Nick was expressing his thanks the door opened and Charles stepped through with a long raincoat in one hand. He must have shaken off most of the wet on the veranda and now hung the coat out to dry in a spot meant for it.

'Good to see you, Nick,' he said, offering a firm handshake. Nick returned the greeting.

'He is joining us for dinner,' Mandy explained at which Charles remarked that it would be their pleasure. During his stay in country Victoria Nick had come to meet a number of fine people. These two were some of the best.

The conversation during the meal opened with a discussion about farming. Nick asked such questions. It had become clear to him long ago that those making a living off the land were actually running a business that required considerable knowledge. Charles farmed beef cattle producing high quality meat due to the animals being contained in well grassed paddocks. Nick's question about breeding led to the topic of marbled meat, a sought after product these days at the top end of the market. It had Charles' interest but would take time. Stock development was a slow process.

After a while Mandy cut in with a comment of her own. 'Sam was asking after you,' she told Nick, 'and sends his regards.'

'How is he?' Nick asked a little surprised. Though he shouldn't be. Sam was the younger of Mandy and Charles' two sons and lived in Melbourne as a university student. Their married daughter was in Perth.

'You mean his studies or his music?' Charles grunted.

Mandy gave her husband an annoyed look. Nick was a musician and apparently a good one. 'Sam's doing well, Nick,' she said.

'Please give him my best wishes,' Nick responded. 'Tell him to drop in when he's around.'

Nick understood Charles' comment perfectly. Few parents would encourage their child into music unless obviously very gifted. Or they might seek to live out their own dreams through their off-spring. Sam, being the extrovert and impulsive person that he was, had arrived at Nick's doorstep one afternoon unannounced in the knowledge that his neighbour was a musician. Nutty had gone wild with pleasure at seeing him again. It was obvious that Sam was fond of the dog. Nick could not help but like the guy. When Sam discovered Nick's actual musical background, that he had been the bass player of a well-known band, he hardly stopped talking. Figuring that his visitor would welcome a jam one day, Nick had invited him to pass by again and bring his guitar. It would give Sam bragging rights with his mates. It was the least he could do for his neighbours' son, Nick felt. Like all young people with a bit of drive and a musical inclination, Sam was a member of a band. Charles need not worry, Nick thought. His son was good on the guitar, but not good enough to make it in the industry. But then, who could tell. At least he would be able to fall back on a tertiary education. That is more than I can do, Nick reflected.

'We have a famous neighbour,' Mandy remarked. 'We had no idea.'

Nick gave her a look. The comment was completely without guile. He thought it best not to answer but took the opportunity of mentioning the reason for his visit.

'Some new prospects in music have come my way recently,' Nick explained. 'It means that I'll be away from the dairy so once in a while. The problem is that I cannot take Nutty with me. I'd rather, but it can't be done. Might she stay with you during my absence?' Nick asked. 'Of course, I'll pay for her keep.'

'No, you won't, Nick,' Charles objected. 'The dog is more than welcome. You're doing me alright with my cattle on your farm. Just call when you'd like to drop her off and pick her up. My dad's dog found herself a fine owner and I'm grateful for that.' Charles seemed adamant on it.

'He's right, Nick,' Mandy joined in. 'I miss that dog more than I thought likely. Just bring her over when you need to, no matter for how long.'

Nick didn't object. Had no intention of doing so. He thanked them sincerely and was waved away with smiles. It would be their pleasure. On his way home, with Nutty once more in the cabin, he reflected on his luck in having Charles and Mandy as neighbours. A plastic container with a large slice of cake rested behind the seats. Mandy's oven exploits for the day.

***

Nick arrived late at the studio in Melbourne due to traffic congestion. Immediately, he was given some clothes to change into by an efficient girl. When newly dressed she led Nick to the make-up chair. His face would be touched up to withstand the scrutiny of intense light. Nick readied himself for a photo shoot. Pictures of *M-Jazz Indigo* were soon to be released into the world of music.

Tom was in discussion with the photographer while Aluka and Jeremy stood in conversation to one side. An attractive woman with short cropped auburn hair wearing baggy pants and a loosely fitting top lingered nearby. She looked amused. One of the studio assistants, Nick presumed. Seen it all before – a bit of theatre. Instead of his jeans he was now wearing dark blue cargo pants, a white T-shirt and light green volleys on his feet. Aluka wore a simple but effective blue dress that obviously was expensive. Jeremy, known as Mr. Chen, looked like an Asian businessman on holidays in his linen suit and pale blue casual shirt. Tom, making sure that there was not to be a complete disconnect from his fame as Vorque, was dressed in black jeans and boots. Plus a silk sliver-grey sleeveless shirt, tailor made, leaving a tattoo on one upper arm visible. He wore a necklace of large wooden beads not unlike a rosary and a thick watch on his wrist. With a good head of longish hair, he had begun growing it again, Tom looked in every way the stylish rocker. It was not an image he would relinquish. Perhaps one day he might reunite with his metal band and tour for a while. Nothing in the music industry should ever be written off as improbable.

Today was indeed theatre, Nick thought. He understood how the colours would blend together with an undertone of blue. The variety of dress styles spoke of sophistication, leisure and adventure with a dark lining. It represented the creativity jazz was known for with a metal edge.

The shoot proceeded as usual. Lights and reflective umbrellas were adjusted often while the group was guided through different poses by their female photographer. There would be a thick pack of shots to choose from in a few days' time. Only a few were needed and those had to be perfect. Tom knew that because of his previous musical success, second rate in anything simply was out of the question. Nick had come to appreciate how much of a businessman his friend actually was. Nothing would be left to chance. Everything was being carefully considered and planned. The success of *M-Jazz Indigo* remained an open question, but it would be given every chance. At the end they were offered refreshments. Nick preferred putting his own clothes back on first. Get the make-up of his face.

Upon return he found the auburn-headed pretty woman giving Tom a big laugh seemingly making fun of him. Not a studio assistant after all, Nick decided. Tom beckoned him over. The woman observed Nick's approach keenly in an approachable way. She was introduced as Tom's sister Georgia, over for a holiday. It took Nick by surprise. He had not heard of her before and she was much younger than her brother. When Tom disappeared into the change rooms, he left Nick and Georgia making small talk.

After the photo shoot they headed for Tom and Aluka's penthouse overlooking the Yarra River. Nick had visited the place before while in Melbourne. Tom preferred to work on *M-Jazz Indigo* musically in Merton. Over the past months the four of them had put in some serious hours on a repertoire. To date it included original compositions and interpretations of well-known ones. People liked to listen to what they already knew but, it being jazz, played in a fresh way. In between you could slot in work exclusively your own. The repertoire of *M-Jazz Indigo* was large enough now to perform in clubs.

Tom suggested they order pizza for dinner. While waiting for their delivery he restated what had been agreed on earlier. The members of *M-Jazz Indigo* would be known as Vorque and Mr. Chen. Nick was to perform under his real name of Nick Avero, while Aluka's stage name would be Aluka Leone. That means lion, Aluka explained, raising her hands as claws with a smile. Any mention of her being Tom's partner should be avoided. Aluka was a musician in her own right without needing association with someone famous.

'I'm looking at a few trial shows before proper gigs,' Tom explained. 'One in Melbourne and in Sydney. Just to test the waters. We'll play sort of unannounced; throw a word into the grapevine, and without pay.'

That sounded like a sensible approach. No-one made comment.

'I'll organise posters with the photos taken today and a CD sleeve for a give-away promo.'

'How many songs on the CD?' Jeremy asked. A recording had been planned, but not the song selection.

'I thought two,' Tom suggested. 'Two of our originals. As you know we will be in the studio next week, in Byron Bay.

'How about the website?' Nick asked.

'Soon to be finished now we have photos. We'll make the CD tracks available as a free download on the website. The gig dates will feature on the site and we'll make a video of the first gig for pieces on YouTube.'

It was the common approach in promoting your band. A music sample to help club owners decide whether to book. With Vorque's fame that would be a lot easier. Plus downloads for promotion. It would encourage people to attend live shows. Things were moving at a pace.

'We should consider vinyl,' Aluka suggested. 'It is the modern trend.'

'We will, later,' Tom responded. 'I would like to hear the quality of our tracks first.'

That would hardly be a problem, Nick thought. The studio at which they were expected was competent. Not of the highest order, for as yet that was unnecessary. They could record in Byron Bay without hitting the limelight. A discussion about which songs to record. Nick had

no preferences and left it to the others to decide. The
pizzas arrived.

Tom took Nick aside.

'Georgia would like to spend some days at my place
in Merton, but I have no time getting her there. Could
she travel up with you tomorrow? Can you look after her
a bit?'

'Sure,' Nick said. 'Does she know about that?'

'I'll ask her.' Tom turned towards his sister with the
suggestion and received a nod of the head.

Georgia came over to discuss the idea with Nick.
She would be grateful for the lift. Nick was glad to be of
help. He wondered about having a female companion in
his car for a few hours. What it would be like. She
seemed nice enough. Memories of Helen flashed through
his mind and he felt his pain badly. These days though
he was less captive to that, which was a relief.

Nick had no idea that Georgia was thinking the same.
Tom would never accept that she had changed her name
to Julian when becoming a religious sister. He would
always call her Georgia. It was fair enough. In Australia,
Julian decided, she would be known as Georgia. It would
be easier and avoided complications. To herself though,
she would remain Julian. It was her name as a religious
sister, which she was.

13

WHAT AN ENORMOUS HOUSE, Julian thought once
again and felt slightly disoriented. It was as if her internal
equilibrium had been disturbed. She was not used to this
kind of space normally living in rather confined quarters
at home in Liverpool. All of her life had been spent in
cities. Now she sat behind a large dining table all alone
gazing through huge windows over the valley below. It
was an unusual feeling. Her bedroom, in the old part of
the house, was not that large. But very comfortable with
enough space for an easy chair and a desk. She had
considered making it her main abode, but decided against
that. It would be foolish to avoid exposure to the open
fields, something she had wished for often. The
experience of country living. Many of the contemplative
writers she had studied seemed to have an affinity for it -
Thomas Merton definitely so. It struck her as ironic that
her brother Tom, whose full name was actually Thomas,
owned a place near a town called Merton. Unlike her
favourite monk from Kentucky, her brother had no time
for his Catholic history. When hearing about his country
retreat she had asked whether she could stay there for a

few days. He had thought of Nick to help with shopping and whatever she needed. Tom had no car at his Merton home.

In her bedroom this morning, Julian had started her day with the daily office. She was now reading at the big table, but could not concentrate. Needed to catch her breath. From a regulated life into being on holidays was a roller coaster of emotions and impressions. Meeting up with Tom had been great. Knowing Aluka, a pleasure. Those two had gone out of their way to make her stay exciting. Showing all kinds of interesting places in Melbourne. Tom was not one for wasting time and always had energy to burn. He was genuinely delighted to have his little sister around. At seventeen he had quit home for music. It had pained him leaving eight year old Georgia behind. He had once told her that. But what could he have done? Nothing! Julian had never held it against him. Not having her big brother close by hurt deeply though. During his travelling life he sporadically kept in touch. When more financial he had sent her a watch for her birthday once. She kept it amongst her possessions all these years. Julian loved her brother, was proud of him, and knew the feeling to be mutual. What an enormous house, she concluded once more.

Yesterday afternoon Nick had dropped her off. She had

asked Tom about Nick and was told that he was a fine guy who could be trusted completely. Not that Julian had doubted that. But what about his sad eyes. Julian was sensitive to people's spirits and in Nick she found shades of depression. When told that his wife had died of cancer quite recently, she had rebuked herself for being that inquisitive. Tom had changed the conversation. He never elaborated on the affairs of others. The few hours' drive with Nick to Merton had been pleasant. It became clear that neither of them were great conversationalists in a car. It seemed to suit both of them. Her reverie was disturbed by the doorbell.

***

Nick had been wondering about Georgia. She certainly was a nice person. But different from any woman he had ever come across. Not that this meant a whole lot. Something about Georgia was rather striking. It had taken him a while to figure it out. Nick had concluded that Georgia seemed rather self-composed for her age, which he guessed to be in the early thirties. As if not much would ruffle her. How true that actually was, he couldn't know. During their drive she had been pleasantly at ease and kind in conversation. If you could call brief comments about the countryside a conversation. He had mostly answered her questions and refrained from asking too many of his own. Whatever Georgia was like, it was not Tom. He was kind as well but hardly restful. There was something else about her. Nick couldn't put his finger on it.

Nick had suggested stopping at the general store in Merton for there might not be much at Tom's for dinner. In any case, Georgia was bound to need milk. They had walked into the shop together with Nick ready to give advice. After all, Merton was not Liverpool and products could differ. Georgia though decided that a tin of quality soup would do for the night and some bread. Nick bought milk and a treat for Nutty. She would be collected on his way to the old dairy. He was looking forward to that. Georgia had been observant enough to notice the purchase and asked about him having a dog. She would certainly meet his kelpie, Nick promised. Presently, Nutty was sitting on the front veranda of Tom's country house while Nick rang the bell. He had promised Georgia to pass by. Help with a proper shop today.

'Glad to see you, Nick.' Julian meant it. Nutty immediately drew her attention. She liked dogs and knelt down to pat this beautiful creature. Nutty was ready to lick her all over but stopped at Nick's command. Even so, her boss seemed pleased about the situation.

'Should she come in?' Julian asked.

'No, she's an outdoors dog,' Nick explained. 'She

likes running around the fields here.'

And would have done plenty of it in the past, Julian figured. 'Come in,' she said. 'I'm sure you know this house better than I do.'

Nick smiled. He liked this undemonstrative woman. She seemed to be at a loss in Tom's place, which surprised him. He expected her to be more self-assured. But then, it was a large home. It might take a while figuring out how everything worked. Yesterday, he had pointed shown her the reverse cycle air conditioning for easy heating. Today he would set up the combustion heater with wood. There was a chill in the air. Quite usual in a house that had been left abandoned for a while.

'You haven't run the aircon,' Nick observed.

'Into bed early,' Julian said. 'Forgot, this morning.'

'Running it is probably better for the house,' Nick suggested. 'Keeps the moisture out, with the piano and all that. I can stoke a fire, but can you keep it burning?'

Julian smiled. 'I'm sure I will be able to throw some wood on.'

'Sorry.' Nick felt a little foolish. 'I'm not usually a male chauvinist,' he apologised.

'I never took you for one,' Julian replied. 'Thanks for caring. Would you like a coffee or tea?'

She busied herself in the kitchen while Nick stacked the heater with wood and put a match to it.

At Merton, Nick showed Julian around town. It was a pleasant place and not large. They walked the streets together and enjoyed each other's company. Nutty heeled all the way. She was well trained, Julian thought. They bought a coffee, sat down at a small table, and discussed what it was like to live in the country. Nick explained what had brought him here. Julian knew about the death of Helen, but did not let on. She sensed that Nick still found it difficult talking about that. His comments that he had been fed up with the city didn't seem quite right. There would be more to the story than that. Nick probably had needed space to grieve alone, away from his past.

Julian explained that in Liverpool, she worked as a special education teacher caring for children with an intellectual disability. It was received with some surprise. As if you needed to be slightly odd to choose such a profession. Not that Nick said so. Julian didn't mind. She was used to this kind of uninformed reaction and found the handsome man with his ponytail sitting across from her good to be with. He was not shy, but hesitant. Perhaps, because he was not used to talking to a woman any more. Or, memories of his wife were playing through his mind. He might be wrestling with an inner conflict. That would be quite understandable, Julian reckoned. It was none of her business. She would leave that side of things well alone.

They purchased enough groceries for a few days. Nick asked whether she would need something from the bottle shop and Julian explained she was not a drinker. Tea, coffee and the rainwater at Tom's place were sufficient. Nutty jumped up into the tray guarding the shopping and they drove back both feeling at ease. Nick, doing the male bit, carried the shopping into the house and placed it on the kitchen bench. Julian began to pack things away.

After a minute she sensed that something about the place was suddenly all wrong. She walked into the main room. Nick was standing with his back to her holding onto a dining table chair for dear life. He stared at the table. His knuckles were white and he back as stiff as a board. It shocked Julian and she quickly came his way.

'Are you alright, Nick?' she asked concerned.

Searching his face she saw nothing but grief and pain. Nick looked intently at her book. *The Revelations of Julian of Norwich* lay on the table from this morning. Tears were welling up in his eyes, which he was trying to fight back.

'I'm sorry,' he mumbled gruffly. 'Sorry. Got to go. Not your fault.'

He seemed to come out of a daze, turned towards the passage way and walked out closing the front door gently behind him.

Julian was stunned. In her short life she had never

been close to so much deep grief before. Poor man, she thought. Whatever had brought this on was serious. Her favourite book seemed at the centre of it. All she could think of was that it concerned Helen somehow. She would pray for Nick. She also felt she should see him again. She wanted to.

At the old dairy Nick put on Black Sabbath loud. He pulled a bottle of whiskey from the kitchen cupboard. Made sure that Nutty had food in her bowl. His eyes watered in coming to grips with what had happened. Seeing that book flooded back memories of Helen's sickbed so vividly, that it instantly destroyed him. So unannounced and with such a vengeance. Nothing could have stopped it though. When will this hurt ever end, he wondered? Staying abreast of it was so difficult. How could it rear its head so badly, even now, well over a year later?

He felt sorry for Georgia being drawn into his misery. Tomorrow he would explain – somehow. Nick had not been drunk for months, but today he was past caring. He looked at Nutty and got the impression that the dog felt sad and helpless. Nothing she could do but be faithful. That book, which Helen had treasured so much, he had no idea what it really was about. That was shameful in a way. But he would never read it. It would be too hard, seeing those pages with many a tick and underlining by Helen. Her face wasted by illness flashed through his mind and her clasping of that book. Nick collapsed. In the end he drank not as much as expected as he had not the energy. The music stopped after an hour and his mind gave up in being conscious. Nick slept hanging sideways in his easy chair with Nutty keeping watch. Later that evening he managed to crawl into bed and slept in a foetal position.

14

'COME IN, NICK,' Julian said with a smile. She was glad to see him again after his surprising departure yesterday. Walking towards the back of the large house, with Nick following a little sheepishly, she turned into the kitchen to brew some coffee.

'Please relax, Nick. We'll talk once I've poured us a cuppa.' By now Julian knew that Nick would never refuse a good coffee. It being brewed, the preparation took some time.

Nick was not at ease. He took the initiative of stoking up the combustion heater. Tom kept plenty of wood close handy and a fair stack next to the fireplace. Soon the flames were burning brightly again. Minutes later Julian arrived at the comfortable seats with a mug of steaming coffee in each hand. Nick thanked her. A strong coffee was just what he needed.

'I owe you an apology,' he said after his first sip looking at the cup in his hand.

'Accepted, Nick. Though I don't feel one is actually needed.' Julian had had him on her mind all morning with inescapable sadness.

'I'd like to explain,' Nick said. He had not expected Georgia to be angry and that turned out right. She did not appear to be that kind of person. But she deserved to hear the reason for his unexpected behaviour.

'Not unless you're comfortable with that, Nick.'

'I am.' Being determined rather than comfortable.

Nick began to tell her why he had seized up so suddenly yesterday. Slowly at first, but progressively he spoke more freely. His story, the one of Helen and the book and her last days, he had not actually ever told to anyone. His grief, from the moment it was discovered that Helen had cancer, had shut him up like a vault. Earlier this morning, thinking it through briefly, he had decided to tell about Helen's dying. Somehow, that seemed right, though he was aware of possibly burdening Georgia. Fortunately, she seemed interested rather than evasive when learning the facts. At one point he had to stop for a while and drunk the last of his coffee.

'Take your time, Nick,' Julian said. 'But please do tell.'

She felt his pain and was almost certain that he had never spoken about this to anyone. Had bottled it up. In a way she felt honoured to be trusted with his story. Of course, her vocation demanded a care in this situation she was only too glad to give. Now was not the time though to tell Nick about her being a religious sister.

Nick, after a few more comments about the funeral and how he had ended up in the country, was nearing the end of the telling. He had mostly been staring into the fire but now looked at his female companion with some hesitation. Should he ask what he had intended to?

Julian saw the uncertainty on his tired face. His eyes were unfocused. Nick was mulling on something, making up his mind.

'Just come out with it, Nick,' she encouraged him. 'If I can help, I will.'

It was the right thing to say. The haze in his eyes vanished and he cleared his throat.

'You know, Georgia, that Julian book, I have no idea what it is about. Helen's copy is in a box somewhere, but I have no heart to read it. I couldn't in my present state of mind. Still, that book gave her so much comfort and I don't know why. That almost seems a sacrilege. As if I am disowning part of her.'

He stopped talking and swallow hard.

'Go on, Nick,' Julian urged. She began to have an idea where this was leading.

Nick gave her another look. She was only in her thirties, he hardly knew her, and he was dumping his grief on her shoulders. Suddenly, that seemed not right. How had it ever come to this? Feeling uneasy he looked away into the fire once more.

'I think, I know what you're asking.' Julian saw him struggling and decided to take the initiative. 'And I have no problem with it. You would like me to tell you what the book is about.'

Nick nodded his head. This was one perceptive lady he was sitting with. He had no idea how much she actually knew about this book. But seeing it yesterday, it seemed to have been much used. Even if he would get the basics, that would be enough.

'I'll get some refills,' Julian suggested. The situation needed a breather and she liked to think matters over.

While making their second mug of coffee Julian wondered what the Lord had got her into. She fingered the little cross around her neck pensively. She carried her own grief but nothing like this. Julian felt out of her depth. Still, she was willing to help where possible. Nick, the more she knew of him, was a fine person. A few thoughts played through her mind about explaining of her favourite book to someone who might find it difficult to appreciate its value. She carried the fresh mugs of coffee to the fireplace. There, Nick was sitting with an exhausted and despondent look on his face. He gave the impression of being embarrassed. Would prefer to take his leave as quickly as possible. That needed addressing, Julian decided. Her special education training was coming in handy. Changing situations for the better.

'Nick,' she said, 'could you please relax. You're as tight as a drum – strung up like a guitar string.'

That got his attention. A smile appeared on his face. She was clever, this Georgia, describing the tension in him in musical terms. He forcefully tried to let go and sunk into the soft cushions of his seat.

'I'll do my best,' he grinned.

'We will have to discuss what you're asking of me,' Julian suggested. 'And don't ever apologise for asking. Is that agreed?'

'Agreed,' Nick said. He would remember that.

'First of all. Helen was a fine Christian now happily in heaven. Otherwise that book would not have interested her. It means little to anyone without Christian beliefs.'

The inference was obvious: what level of faith did Nick have? He stroked his forehead with one hand as if to smooth the wrinkles away. It was a question he might have expected and should face up to.

'I'm not at all scrutinising your faith, Nick,' Julian explained warmly. 'It's just that unless you understand what faith entails, you will never really come to see how Helen received her spiritual strength from that book. How others might in their particular circumstances.'

Julian had no idea about Nick and Christian beliefs. But Helen was unlikely to have married someone averse to it. That was correct. Nick explained his faith to be on a slow burner because of what had happened to him. Who could blame him for that, Julian concluded.

'That leaves the matter of how much time we shall have for me to explain Julian of Norwich without always having to talk about her. Neither you nor I would want that. We'll just have to see. There should be enough for you to hear the basics.'

Nick agreed wholeheartedly. After all, Georgia was on holidays. A brief explanation was all he needed.

'I am coming to Byron Bay. So we'll be together for a while. You may get sick of me.' A little humour would not go astray, Julian felt.

Nick smiled. Tiring of Georgia was unlikely. He had not known about Byron Bay and was pleased.

There was one other point. Julian gave that some thought. How to phrase her next comment.

'You've told me about Helen. Her strength in such a horrible time. I can explain the encouragement she found from that book. But I have no idea what she looked like. I don't know the kind of person she was, though I can guess. You need to help me there. I cannot talk about Helen and ideas precious to her as if she were a stranger.'

Nick nodded. Helen had remained hidden in his memories exclusively for too long. It was time to bring her out into the open. Georgia was right.

'I have a picture on the wall of my kitchen,' Nick said. 'Why don't you come along for lunch?' This spontaneous suggestion surprised him. He had not considered it before.

'Glad to, Nick,' Julian said. 'I'll just get a jacket.'

She looked forward to finding out where this friend of Tom's and his dog lived. For all his sadness, or partly because of it, Nick was an interesting person.

The moment the old dairy came in view, Julian knew she liked the place. The way it sat in green undulating hills with large old trees spread about. When they stopped in the yard Nutty jumped from the tray and was off down the paddock where the creek ran through. She might have seen a fox Nick explained or whatever. The dog would return soon enough. Julian took her time in following Nick towards the back of the house getting a feel of her surroundings. Old with character, a real estate agent might have decided. Clearly work had been done recently to spruce things up.

On their drive in, which had left them both with their private thoughts, Nick decided not to apologise for what was home. Undoubtedly his was a bachelor pad and lots could be done to improve it. The kitchen was old as was the plumbing. But everything was functional and quite comfortable. All he had done inside was making sure of enough light in the right places for a pleasant mood. An electrician had sorted that out and Nick was happy with the result. A few extra power points also came in handy. When he opened the kitchen door he took a deep breath. He hoped Georgia would like his home. Somehow that seemed important. What people expected from a good home was distinctly personal. You never really knew.

He need not have worried. The visitor on holiday from England did like it and very much so. She was quick in showing her appreciation. Julian noticed the quote from Julian of Norwich, *Alle Shalle Be Wele,* hanging up. She didn't comment. Nick stood near the dresser for her to finish looking around. He took a picture off the wall that was hanging out of sight and handed it over. Julian looked intently at an intelligent pretty face with medium-long blond hair. The eyes were smiling and at rest. She felt a small jolt of recognition. She had never met Helen, nor ever would, but detected a kindred spirit. Julian looked at Nick and nodded. He turned away towards the stove for cooking lunch.

'I'm out of bread,' he explained. He had not expected a visitor. 'How about bacon and eggs with baked beans, or do you prefer cheese and crackers?'

'Eggs will be great,' Julian agreed. That actually would make a nice lunch.

Nick stoked up the Aga adding wood and left the kitchen. Julian heard him scurrying about in another room. She sat down at the table carefully placing Helen's picture to one side. When Nick returned he carried a photo book.

'Look through these,' he suggested. 'Rainwater with lemon, tea, coffee or a beer, what would you prefer?'

Julian settled for water while Nick took a stubby of beer from the fridge and began cooking lunch.

The photos depicted a holiday Nick and Helen had taken in Vietnam. One of those books you could arrange on the internet inserting your own pictures. It confirmed what Julian already knew. Helen and Nick had been happy. A picture tells a thousand words. She felt slightly like an intruder, a voyeur, but that was nonsense. Nick seemed not hesitant in her having a look and she was interested. When lunch was ready, Julian felt to have a good idea of Helen. Eating away at their leisure, Nick explained how he met her at a friend's party. About Helen being a chemist, and of her deep interest in Christian spirituality. Helen had been light-hearted without being superficial. Was not easily flustered, trusting that matters would sort themselves out.

'Would you like me to show you around outside,' Nick suggested, eventually. 'We can walk off the calories.'

'I'd love that, Nick,' Julian said. She meant it.

With Nutty in tow they meandered through the gates and paddocks with owner Nick explaining about the land and answering her questions. At a log near a rapid in the creek they sat down. Julian could see for miles. Nick suggested she listen to the birds. They were chirping all over the place once competing with the harsh sound of a crow. What a gorgeous place, Julian thought. She liked it better than Tom's beautiful home. It felt earthy and close to nature.

15

JULIAN WAS THINKING. She sat at the breakfast bar of the kitchen munching her muesli and looked out of the window towards some trees in the distance. On her way back from the old dairy, she had promised Nick to email him a copy of the notes from her talk months ago – the idea of *Julian's Windows*. It had been sent last night. After setting up an address as Georgia. She had suggested he consult the net about Julian of Norwich for that would offer ample information. It would help, Julian had thought. She expected that Nick for all his desire to know about that book, as he called it, would soon tire of extensive detail. Nor would she enjoy her time with him when continually discussing spiritual theology.

She had come to Australia on holidays to consider the question of her vocation. Whether to take her vows once again. The discussion with the community leader had been amiable. In no sense had she been dissuaded from finding her own answer. Or been encouraged towards remaining a religious sister. Years of experience had taught the church that was counterproductive. She had been urged to focus her question in prayer. That was obvious and advice readily taken. She had prayer and less so lately. Jesus took pleasure from prayer petitions, but was not demanding. The Lord would know her request. Possibly was the instigator of it.[45] She had felt free to rest from her search resting in faith.

Permission for visiting family had been granted with her leave delayed because of school commitments. As Tom was the only family member she cared to be with, an overseas trip was allowed. From the moment she stepped on the plane in London, she had experienced a freedom of spirit not felt for ages. Everyone she met was looking after her well and her holiday time was invigorating. That included the surprises Nick put her way, which in no sense were a burden. Rather, it brought greater understanding. Being exposed to the unremitting reality in which people simply managed without the security of a large institution. The price you paid for that safety was relinquishing much of your freedom. A caring place to live out your vocation was what you gained.

About finding an answer to her future? Nothing had settled within her spirit beyond what she already knew. Should she forego the joys and aches of motherhood? Not that a life without children was second rate. It could be well lived. Still, the dilemma facing her persisted and had not lost its urgency. The memory of that mother and her child on the little one's birthday flashed through her mind. She almost felt that ache again.

If she were honest, the real question was different still. It was central to motherhood, but not something she could do much about. She had pushed it aside knowing well what the answer should be. These last two days this question had begun to gain an unexpected urgency. Would she be willing to fall in love? Her bad memories of that time with Mark as a student still grated. What he had taken from her.

Actually, the real question was different still. Was she falling in love right now, perhaps? Was that happening to her? Though early days, the answer probably was – yes! The predicament about her vows had found no answer as an inner conviction. It appeared that she was receiving it through feelings instead. Julian smiled ruefully. The Lord could be full of surprises.

Long ago she had decided not to fool herself in anything, if that were possible. How she felt about life as it moved on. She recognised the tug on her heart for what it might be and wondered. It was not as if she had been looking for this. The suddenness of it all was confusing. It made her question whether she was reading her emotions correctly. Last night she had gone to bed with the idea of sleeping it off. Perhaps in the morning her emotions might have settled down. Clearly, that was not the case.

From meeting Mark, Julian had learned that love could arrive fast and out of nowhere. Might be volatile and unpredictable. Now many years later, and surely wiser, she would keep a cooler head. Her present feelings reminded of those student days. That keen desire to reach out and be with someone. She knew it to be a good emotion and reflective of God. Julian of Norwich had seen God's deep longing towards connecting with every person. A thirst that will not be quenched until heaven is complete. All because of God's searching love.[46] Falling in love partially revealed the nature of God.

Love is the primary force in our universe, Julian believed. It manifests in many ways. All that is good in the world originates from God's love. Good is a derivative of eternal love. A simple act of caring is essentially an expression of love. Though many people would not see it so. A good deed, it is a manifestation of the dynamic of love in our world. But that deep desire for another, and it being reciprocated, that was what people considered the real nature of love to be like. That was the experience everyone was looking for.

She should be careful. Nick must not get hurt. He carried more than enough of that around already. She must not let her feelings show. For a start, they might well change over time. Perhaps she was overreacting to his sad story with a kind of motherly urge. But she didn't think so.

And of course, she was still a nun. Telling Nick about her vocation had to wait. It only confused matters. While she herself should not be overly mindful of being a religious sister. It would complicate love. There was no need, for soon she might leave the order anyway.

I'm getting way ahead of myself, Julian thought, washing her bowl in the kitchen sink. She made her way to the bathroom. When looking into the mirror above the vanity basin she had a strange sensation. Something about her eyes had changed. Also, she noticed an emotional pull within her that was unnerving. A sense of womanhood she had never felt before, definitely not with Mark. Oh, my good Lord, she thought, and recognised it as a song line of George Harrison. She would need to be careful.

The phone rang. It would be Tom, who checked up on her daily.

***

Nick needed a chainsaw. Usually he bought his split wood for a fire locally but the trees on his property carried branches that were better lopped off. It would supply ample firewood. If he could be bothered cutting and splitting it. He was not keen on those types of saws and considered them potentially dangerous. Still, was he a man or a mouse? Country people used chainsaws. A guy with a dairy and trees was silly not to own one. The place he had in mind for buying a saw was in Mansfield. Perhaps Georgia might be happy to come along. He had dropped her off home yesterday secure in the knowledge of not having over-burdened her. She had made it clear more than once how much she was enjoying herself. A phone call earlier this morning had confirmed her acceptance. Mansfield was close to Mount Buller, a well-known ski resort. They would drive up there for lunch. It was well before the snow season though.

Nick had constructed a travel box for Nutty. Being mostly plastic with a wire mesh door the box was easily lifted the tray and tied down. It kept Nutty out of the weather when driving. A thick old blanket on the floor for comfort. She never liked being in that box, but soon settled. At Mansfield Nick told her to heel. The kelpie heeled behind the nice lady from England, perhaps making a point about travelling in that box. Nutty's behaviour actually pleased Nick. He left them to walk the main street, while he would make his purchase.

Nick entered a shop that sold motorcycles, mowers and saws. Not knowing a great deal about saws buying one would not be quick. Soon he was talking it over with the store owner. Because Mansfield was in a large area of wooded mountain country the selection of saws was considerable. Nick decided on size and quality. It was followed by instructions on how to operate and maintain the saw: What type of fuel and lubricating oil to use. How to keep the tension on the chain and to sharpen the teeth. He bought the needed accessories and locked his purchase inside the cabin of his car to prevent theft. If ever he found using his saw a problem, he could always ask Charles. Nick was confident that would not be necessary.

Julian was happy about Nick asking her along. She was taking to this wonderful country like a duck to water. How restrictive had her existence in Liverpool been, really? For city people it was fine. That she had imagined herself to be. Now she discovered otherwise. She would stay alert and try not to miss anything that drew her attention. Whether walking or driving around with Nick in his small truck. Tomorrow, they would leave for Melbourne and a flight to Byron Bay the day after. It was all too soon.

Mansfield, in Victoria's high country, was a sizeable town. It had a wide main street that featured a grassed strip at its center. Many of the streets in old towns were wide because in years gone by it allowed for bullock carts to turn around in them, Nick had told her. She walked along the shops, some with old style gables. Mansfield was a tourist town with a horse riding history. Mountain biking and skiing were popular at Mount Buller.

When Nick caught up, he ambled along explaining about the town. He asked whether she had bought something in the shops yet. Julian took her time selecting a souvenir for her community. Nick was holding his patience. Well done, Nick, she complimented him amused. With Nutty he was waiting on the sidewalk. He raised his eyebrows with a smile. There was a chill in the air. But the breeze blew only softly.

They drove up to the Mount Buller ski resort for lunch. The drive was lovely, if you liked mountains. Seeing a few kangaroos close to the road Julian excitedly asked him to stop. She would take a photo. Farmers thought them a nuisance, Nick mused. As did insurance companies. But they surely drew in the tourists. The car wound up the mountain slowly taking many a twist and turn in following the bitumen. In winter this would only be possible using snow chains. The resort with its ski lifts offered fabulous views over mountains far and wide. Julian stepped out of the car and took a deep breath. How good was this?

16

NICK FOUND A RESTAURANT with a view and the promise of fine food. There were always people about at Mount Buller, today being no different. But fewer than in the snow season by far. Today many sported a mountain bike. A window table was readily available. Julian spent the ample time taking in the scenery. The mountains and a few ski lifts in sight. She studied the menu and asked Nick for advice. He explained that the fish on offer might have arrived frozen rather than fresh. Not so the meat, most likely. He would ask about that. Julian settled for rack of lamb while Nick looked forward to a steak. Both straight from the butcher this morning. Soda water for Julian and a beer for Nick.

He observed his new friend while she took in the view once more. Again today, no make-up on her pretty face. She carried a healthy tinge from being outdoors. Looked even better than when they had first met some days ago. Julian noticed Nick's attention and reminded herself to be careful. If all was as it might be, it would have to wait a fair while yet.

They talked about Mount Buller, a Mecca for hikers and bikers. What it was like when thick under snow. Lunch arrived and the food was very tasty. Their time together relaxing. They got on well. During a period of silence Nick said thanks for the email about Julian of Norwich.

'You haven't read it yet, I suppose,' Julian asked with a smile. Had not expected him to.

Nick shook his head. It needed a suitable time.

'I've given our talk of yesterday some more thought,' Julian explained. 'Thanks for sharing about Helen and the photos. That was important to me.'

She looked at Nick, who now was gazing at his beer. The mention of Helen cut through his carefree mood. It confirmed the difficulty Julian had perceived.

'Listen, Nick,' she said gently. 'Yesterday, I promised to show you how Helen might have engaged with the information of that book, positively engaged. And I will. At least the main ideas.'

Nick nodded.

Julian looked out of the window searching for the right words.

'But I will do so leaving Helen out of it. You can make up your mind about how the information might have shaped Helen's thinking and feeling.'

Nick kept staring at his glass. When he raised his head, he gave her a smile.

'You know, Georgia. I know what you're saying.'

Julian's emotions tumbled about. Seeing this nice guy who carried such hurt. It would not be healthy if whenever they talked about Lady Julian the memory of Helen came in play. It would, but by not mentioning Helen that could be minimised.

'Could you please get me another soda water, Nick?' she asked. It broke the flow of their talking and she could do with a fresh drink.

'Rather than coffee?' he suggested, getting up.

'Rather.'

As Julian expected, Nick arrived with a soda water and his coffee.

While buying the drinks Nick tried to get Helen out of his mind. He should concentrate on his companion rather. It seemed, he would have to live with both, in his thinking that was. His focus to be on Georgia, but Helen would be present in a nonintrusive way. It was a new experience for him. He would never mention it. But Georgia was too astute not to notice. She had shown an ability to read such situations a number of times already.

'What do you know about mysticism?' Julian asked.

'Nothing,' Nick had to admit.

'Mostly,' Julian continued, 'mystics receive insights about God and the divine realm by special revelation.

This happened to Julian of Norwich on a sickbed in three ways.'

Nick waited, wondering where this was leading.

'She had bodily visions, which means that what see saw appeared to be as real as you and I talking here today. She had intellectual visions, which she explained as words forming in her understanding. And, she was given spiritual visions.[47] She received ideas and impressions, spiritually very real, but of a kind that are difficult to put into words. Words are simply insufficient. It is a problem common to all mystics. The divine realm is open to a perception that is way beyond intellectual interpretation. So, you will end up with seers making the best of relating their encounters. They can never arrive at fully satisfactory descriptions.'

Wow, Nick thought, Georgia seemed to have a good handle on this. For some obscure reason, that really pleased him.

'Julian of Norwich faced another problem as well. Some of what she understood did not easily align with church teaching at that time. It made her wonder. The Lord encouraged her to remain faithful to the church, while accepting that his ways will be higher than those of the Church and at times her own beliefs.[48] It is suggested that becoming an anchoress enabled her to write out her understanding without the danger of being declared a heretic. No-one, not even the Bishop, was allowed to enter her cell ever, until her death.'

Nick sat back looking at his friend.

'You may be wondering why I'm explaining this. The extent to which Lady Julian went in making sure that her visons could be correctly recorded, testifies to the integrity of her writings. It can't be pushed aside as mere excessive imagination. Thomas Merton rated her amongst England's best theologians ever.'

Nick remembered that name from a few of Helen's books.

'Julian herself began to question whether what she has seen had been no more than hallucinations due to illness. But the Lord told her otherwise.'[49]

Julian took a sip of her soda water.

'The point is, Nick,' she continued, 'that when taking to heart what Julian of Norwich saw, you are not chasing an illusion, rather you are discovering true reality. Not everything the anchoress said is that crystal clear. It is a problem common to all mystics. And to get the full picture you must never settle on the acceptance of an idea from one chapter if it is also discussed in another perhaps with extended perspectives. Also, related issues need to be considered.'

Don't overload your points, Julian thought. She was close to sounding like a university lecturer. Nick was looking at her rather impressed.

'Sorry, Nick,' Julian apologised. 'I just got carried

away. All I'm saying is that what Helen would have taken from the book, she could safely accept as true and believe in it, and so can you.'

Nick was surprised by the depth of knowledge he was exposed to more so than by its verbosity. He figured that Georgia was trying to keep it simple and concise. But not everything in life was that simple. Mysticism was complex.

'You're doing okay, Georgia,' he said with a smile, and meant it.

Julian smiled back. He was such a gorgeous man.

'I'll be brief then,' she said.

This introduction needed something practical.

'In essence, the revelations we are talking about, are about love and suffering. The love and suffering of God and that of people.[50] God is love. God is also very close if we care to accept that and reach out for that reality.[51] And the nature of that nearness Julian of Norwich saw as being homely, as familiar.[52] Jesus is very courteous, easily approached and kind. He fully identifies with what is happening to us including our suffering.[53] He helps us through, helps us overcome whatever the difficulty whether sickness or temptation.[54] His familiarity does not make him our mate, as you Australians call someone you really get on with. More a majestic friend who willingly divests of his status to relate simply and without decorum. Lady Julian was adamant though that this should not lead to us dropping a sense of reverence. She called it fear, though to us that word involves the idea of apprehension, which is unnecessary when a Christian approaches Jesus.[55] When trouble hits us in this life there is no better answer than knowing Jesus to be present as familiar and powerful. It does not change your problems as such, but it places them in a different light. Adding a perspective that helps you cope better. It might even be, that those problems help you understand God better. That sense of reaching out and entering a realm of spiritual understanding you did not have before. However strange it may sound, it can even enlarge your love for God. But I'm not suggesting that this always happens.'

Nick understood that though she spoke easily, Georgia put in an effort. She was honouring her promise and might have preferred just sitting together making small talk. He still felt that his request about that book was intruding into her holidays. It had been an impulsive response to an emotional few hours. His new friend from England was looking out of the window again.

Julian sensed deflation settling on her. Just like after a hard day's work trying to help children with disabilities without great success. She knew it was a wrong assessment, but who could prevent feelings.

'Georgia,' Nick said gently, getting her attention.

'Thanks.'

He gave her another smile.

'That was very helpful, to know what Helen saw and understood when she was so sick. I had no real idea of it. Even though I figured something like what you explained was happening.' He had to leave it at that.

Julian saw him struggle. She had no words to lessen Nick's plight and remained silent. Her momentary little deflation meant nothing compared with what this man had faced and still was coping with.

Nick made a final comment.

'Please don't think that I would tire of learning about that book. That's all I can say. You are great at explaining things.'

For a moment he looked destitute and then gathered his faculties. It was time to get a move on.

'Thanks, Nick,' Julian said. And she gave him the warmest smile he had received from her yet.

Oh, my good Lord, she thought.

***

The next day Nick arrived at Tom's hide-away for Julian's lift to Melbourne. Nutty was at his side. He explained that the dog would be dropped off at his neighbours' farm. They always looked after her when he was away. She had been the dog of the farmer's father. Meeting Charles and

Mandy would give Julian further idea of country life.

Soon they arrived. Nick had called last night. He found both his neighbours in the kitchen and introduced Georgia. It appeared that Charles had been waiting for him to lend a hand with a small job. The two men disappeared into the shed.

Mandy, her friendly good self, soon had the visitor from England sitting at the kitchen table with a cup of tea and home-baked biscuits. She had scrutinised this attractive young woman unobtrusively, a fact that did not escape Julian. If these folk were Nick's friends, he was fortunate. Julian had a good sense for people. How good a friend they actually were, became clear from Mandy's next comment. She too had sat down at the table.

'I know it's rude, none of my business, but I'll say it anyway.' Mandy decided that with Charles and Nick soon to be back, there was no time for a lead-in conversation.

That got Julian's attention. She saw a kind, strong and intelligent woman sitting across.

'Please deal with Nick carefully. You're his type and very attractive. He might fall for you and get badly hurt without that being your intention.' Mandy observed her visitor with interest. How this would be received. She hid her unease at speaking so directly.

Julian understood the concern. Annoyance flashed through her mind but she arrested it. Mandy cared about her neighbour more than he would know, she gathered. That thought prevented her putting up defences.

Mandy smiled apologetically.

'I appreciate that you care about Nick,' Julian said. 'I understand your concern. I won't lead him on.'

'Thank you,' Mandy said simply, relieved at the non-aggressive response. 'He's a fine man. I'm not suggesting that you should avoid him. How long will you be around for?'

'A few days.' Julian made sure to speak warmly.

'And then back to England?'

'Yes.'

Mandy was impressed. Nick's new friend was a quality person. If those two would ever get together, it would be good news. She had a premonition, but who could tell.

'If we meet again, one day,' Mandy said, 'it will be a pleasure.'

'Thank you.' Julian hoped that they would.

The kitchen door opened with Charles and Nick walking through. 'Time for a coffee,' Charles declared. He wouldn't mind quietly getting the measure of this lady Nick had brought along. She seemed nice enough. With a fresh brew in front of everyone and pleasant conversation, the time to say goodbye arrived quickly.

17

JULIAN WAS WALKING through Byron Bay with an amused smile on her face. The town had outgrown its hippy history, but still teemed with tourists from all over the world. If you visited Australia, Byron Bay was high on the bucket list. Mostly for younger people, but all ages were represented.

Julian enjoyed looking at how everyone was dressed. In Liverpool the weather was often cool to cold and people dressed accordingly. In Byron Bay today it was mild with a slight drizzle in the air. Soon the sunshine would break through. Everyone was dressed for the sun with plenty of bare flesh on show. It was an interesting display of individuality and identity consciousness. Julian made a fine time of ambling around in the midst of it all.

The environment was lush, more tropical than Melbourne. The streets were lined with small shops and eating places. Nothing in the centre of town was large apart from a few pubs. That would be on purpose, Julian presumed. The place had a market feel about it and sat on a beautiful beach that came in view if you walked up hill.

When browsing through the streets and side alleys, sea and sand were invisible. Byron Bay spread a fair way along the coast with many homes hidden amongst abundant green vegetation. Julian had discovered that when driving in from Lennox Head, about half an hour south. Tom had hired two comfy cars and left earlier this morning for a second day in the studio. The other car was at Julian's disposal.

Yesterday, she had wiled the time away doing nothing special. Just sitting on the wooden deck of a large rented house a few kilometres inland from Lennox. It was built on a hill with views over the ocean far away. In the morning, if up early, you could see the sun rise over the sea. Tom didn't like Byron Bay. Nor did he wish to be recognised as Vorque in that international location. Nick had played a number of times there with his previous band and seen enough of the place. Jeremy stayed with friends at Byron, as the locals called it, and made his way to the studio from there.

Julian had been encouraged to pay the famous town a visit. It was completely different from Lennox Head, a cute village along a beautiful beach. She had ambled along the foreshore there yesterday and through the sand near the water watching some surfers trying to make the best of average waves. She had no idea about surfing, but according to Tom with really good waves the place would be packed with board riders.

She liked Lennox Head. Julian liked Australia. The sky was never closed in above your head. Australia gave the impression of lots of space and freedom under the sun, moon and stars. Wait till you travel about and get to the interior, Tom had said. I will show you the outback if ever you come again. Not that he expected that to happen any time soon.

Julian made her way up the incline that led to Byron Bay beach. She found a place for a coffee and a look around. Nick had got her onto coffees. The whole of Australia seemed one large coffee culture. Here I sit, she thought philosophically, a single person in a wide universe amongst lots of other people busy like ants in seeking to find significance. To a large extent tourism was about just that. But an anchored significance was an inner quality, Julian reflected. Modern life with its continuous impressions, distractions and temptations, was not very conducive to inner unity. Deep inside most people maintained a mild turmoil. Relational engagements with real meaning were a key. You needed to give, when seeking inner significance and a solid sense of identity.

Nick came to mind, but her reverie was disturbed by a handsome guy of about her own age. He wore leathers and a black t-shirt with a Harley symbol on his chest. Proffering a brochure, he looked disgustingly healthy and was an extrovert. A man for the ladies and he knew it.

'Would you like to see Byron on a shining motorbike today?' he asked handing her a colourful pamphlet.

Julian had to smile. She couldn't help herself.

'I do day trips and night trips.'

He gave this attractive woman with her nice figure an appraising look. All wholesomeness, he decided. No need for dressing up to look good. Experience told him there might be deep waters hidden within the female sex. Secret desires often unacknowledged. Sometimes you could tell, but often not. Holidays tended to loosen them up.

'Night trips can be special, including visiting clubs and so.'

What 'and so' meant, was left to the imagination. Julian kept smiling in anticipation of his reaction.

'Why would I do that?' she said. 'I'm a nun.'

The biker burst out laughing. He was one of those people who would never be bothered by female rejection knowing there were plenty of willing others. 'I'll give you that one,' he said grinning. 'Anyway, if you change your mind my number is on that brochure. I've got a beautiful bike that needs a gorgeous lady.' With that he left shaking his head. On his way to finding his next customer.

Julian stared out over the sea and tried coming to grips with the encounter. It should be water on a duck's back, but it wasn't. She had felt flattered by this conversation, however superficial. It was a pleasant feeling. She didn't look like the typical nun. Few religious sisters gave that impression these days. But that guy and his flirtation had stirred something that she should better keep at bay. The primal urge of humanity, analysed by Freud and others, had powerful undercurrents. I'm beginning to feel less like a nun all the time, Julian thought. More like a Georgia. She needed to find her car – start walking.

When she arrived back at the house, her mind was in a muddle. Sitting with a glass of water on the large deck she gave the last few days some thought. She was glad to have set up an email account as Georgia. It avoided connection with Talitha Cumi or her community. She had no idea how much Nick would be in touch with her back in England. She was still adamant in keeping her real feelings for him hidden. Any contact needed to be as Georgia at a private address.

The idea of discussing Julian of Norwich was losing traction. Their conversations were not that many and unsuitable for theological discourse. Before flying back to Liverpool, she would like to leave Nick a few more insights on how Helen might have found her strength in such times of trouble. Caring for Nick felt like paying her dues to Helen. It was irrational but a real feeling.

Julian thought of writing a short story for him to

muse over. It would be based completely on the teachings of Lady Julian, but unlike how the anchoress had written. At least that will focus my mind, Julian thought.

Agapino

Agapino, a beautiful little angel, appeared before God in heaven and was received with much delight. 'You're looking tired, Agapino,' the Lord observed.

'It's hard work spreading love about on earth, Lord,' the little angel confessed.

'You tell me about it,' the Lord agreed.

'I have to fight all that suffering and pain. It's difficult to pierce through that and make love relevant.'

'Yes, but you know the pain has to be, I'm afraid.' It was not the first time God had told the little angel this. 'Just wait till you see for yourself where it is leading. I will explain that to everyone one day.'[56]

'I know you will do a great deed Lord, far greater than anyone can ever imagine. It will make all things well.'[57]

Agapino had no problem with that. Whatever the Lord said, it would be so.

'Oh yes!' God confirmed. 'Do you remember my servant Job, whom you tried to encourage? He was blessed doubly after all his suffering.'

'It was not of much help to him while he sat in

ashes,' Agapino observed carefully.

'No, not then,' God had to admit. 'It hurt him, and me a lot. But it had to be.'

There was a moment of reflective silence in heaven.

'Some people I cannot reach,' Agapino reported. 'They know not love,'

'Some are of the devil's condition,' God explained. 'Don't waste your time there. I won't have them mentioned in my sight.'[58].

Agapino let that be.

'Most of them I find just have been blinded,' the little angel concluded. 'What they are really looking for I can offer, but they ignore me.'[59]

'You will have to suffer that Agapino. Keep working on a breakthrough,' God insisted. 'All the blind I keep alive within my heart. I hold them dear.'[60]

'Even though, they are fallen?' Agapino questioned.

'I don't blame them for it.[61] That is our problem – Mine, my Servant Son[62] and our Spirit. It has been solved.'

'They all have fallen, Lord,'

'They all live in my heart – apart from those of the devil, who are but a few.'

'How about those who have Jesus as their Saviour,' Agapino asked knowing the answer. The angel just took delight in hearing it.

'You know full well Agapino,' God answered with

pleasure. 'Those are special. Not only are they in my heart, I dwell within theirs in a wonderful way.'[63]

'But even Christians can be hopeless with love, Lord,' the little angel complained.

'Come on, Agapino, straighten your back.' God smiled warmly. 'You must always take pleasure from those who understand salvation. I do.'

'Some understand it well,' Agapino had to admit. 'They can see love even when in pain.'

'They are my treasure,' God said. 'They know that I'm hurting with them. They will just have to trust that I will make all things very well one day.

'Others don't live in accordance to what they confess though,' Agapino ventured.

'They should know better.'

'But you are not angry about that?

'Angry? Have you ever seen anger in me, Agapino?'[64]

The little angel shook the head.

'My wrath is simply displeasure and a display of holiness, but it is not anger.' God was adamant on that. 'My wrath is because I love them and they behave stupidly.'

'So you are also not angry with those who don't know you?'

'How can I be angry, if anger is not me, nothing like who I AM, Agapino?'

'So you have a place for them somewhere?'

'I have a place for almost everybody. The first fruits, those who truly serve me while living on the earth, they will have their special rewards.'[65]

The little angel looked at God. Perhaps too many questions were being asked. God, however, had divine patience.

'When people are hurting, they don't like me,' Agapino tried once again, for sympathy's sake.

'Often they don't like me either, and I AM God,' was the answer.

'So what do I tell everyone?' the angel of love persisted.

'What I've told you many times, Agapino.' God looked at the little servant kindly.

'That you love them more than they can ever know, and that counts almost everybody in.'

God nodded.

'That you understand their suffering and suffer likewise.[66] They just have to try accepting that.'

God nodded.

'That you look after those who have died.'

God nodded.

'And that you take great pleasure in those who are reaching out for you during their earthly lives. You are willing to be a friend to them.'[67]

God nodded. 'I'm closer than their breathing.'[68]

'That's good news, Lord,' Agapino said.

'You've got it, my little friend. You've got it.' God smiled. 'Go with speed on your way. Keep the chin up.'

Julian took pleasure from writing this story. She felt close to God right now and easily accepted that real anger and God did not mix even though the Bible used the word at times. Anger was a human experience, and fundamental. It covered many shades of feeling. Its essence was destructive and an outcome of sin. That kind of anger could not be reconciled with God. If God was actually ever angry, it had to be a pure anger devoid of negativity and spite. People viewed anger differently. Therefore the notion of an angry God presented a wrong picture of God's nature. A much better word would be displeasure about an excessive lack of holiness and goodness in people's behaviour. God's 'anger' was a level of displeasure that needed a response. The Bible used the word wrath for such a situation. But it would be a holy wrath always be tempered by love. Even though this might not seem to be so. Essentially, God is love first and foremost, Julian reflected. She always took great comfort from that understanding.

***

That evening Julian sat with Tom on the deck in twilight looking out towards the sea. Nick had gone to Lennox

Head to buy beer. Joined by Aluka, who needed to visit the chemist.

'It's been great having you around, Georgia.' Tom gave his religious sister a pensive look. 'I'll miss you.'

Julian would fly out the day after tomorrow.

'And I won't be the only one,' Tom continued.

'You mean, Nick?' Julian asked carefully.

'Yeah, Nick,' Tom said. 'I realise that you could hardly be unfriendly, but still.' The difficulty Tom perceived, he did not mention.

'Tom,' Julian said. 'Please, look at me.' She loved her brother.

Her tone of voice caught his attention.

'I will be leaving the order.'

Confusion briefly played all over his face and then an enormous smile.

'I came visiting to get clarity about my vows. Give myself time away from Liverpool.'

Tom took a sip of his drink just to allow for this great news to settle in.

'And you got more clarity than you bargained for,' he surmised perceptively.

Julian nodded. 'Yes, I did.' She smiled ruefully. 'Nick knows nothing about me being a nun and should not find out. I don't want a relationship till after leaving the order. You mustn't tell anybody.'

'I'm the only one here who knows,' Tom explained,

'about your vocation.'

'Nick can find me in England. If ever he wants to.'

'Oh, he will.' Tom was convinced. 'Though I'm not sure he knows that.'

Julian didn't comment. She felt not certain that Nick would come to Liverpool. Tom's next remark increased the likelihood though.

'There is a possibility that *M-Jazz Indigo* will play in London in three months' time,' he told her and paused.

'Hey, Sis – welcome back.' Tom raised his glass.

Julian looked at him and understood.

'When I was so busy becoming famous, I hardly had time to see you. Once I had more time, you had become a nun. I respect that. But boy it put a spanner into the works of us seeing each other.'

Tom stopped talking. Julian saw him choke up, just a little.

'Give me a hug, sis,' he suggested getting up from his chair.

She was hugged by a man as never before. Tom almost squeezed the life out of her. Julian had known nothing about his hurt from missing his little sister. He had protected her from it. She could not help it and burst into tears on his shoulder. Memories and regrets came flooding in of a childhood and a youth alone, without Tom. Oh Georgia, he mumbled softly. After a while she settled and he still just held her, like a big brother does.

18

THEIR LAST DAY at Lennox Head, Tom and Aluka left for the studio to appraise the recording, discuss the mix, and tidy up the music if necessary. Nick was no longer needed having played the bass to everyone's satisfaction. Jeremy was flying back to Sydney this morning. It allowed Nick a free day. He suggested they visit Bangalow. Julian happily agreed. It would be the last day of her holidays. Tomorrow morning they were to fly out from Ballina to Melbourne with her connection to London following on that evening. A short drive along the highway north with a turn off left into the hills had them arrive at Bangalow midmorning. Mostly one major street that ran uphill and was lined with small shops. Some funky, others expensive, Julian concluded. There was the pub, noticeably situated midway. Nick explained that on Sundays a street market attracted a lot of people. Today it was quiet. Together they ambled along in the balmy weather. Nick, it seemed, had decided to be as accommodating as he could with regard to browsing in the various shops. Julian took her time in selecting a shawl asking him which one suited her best. Anything will suit you Georgia, he had commented with a smile, but settled on the one she liked best herself. Julian was determined to put her journey home tomorrow out of her mind.

The pub offered an open veranda at the back where they settled for a light meal. Nick was happy with a bowl of potato wedges and Julian a salmon baguette. Nick looked tired, she noticed. Music could be hard work. Particularly, when recording and you needed the right expression from your instrument. Always, there was the energy factor. Good music, whether loud or soft, was much determined by the energy that is projected. A kind of tension that made the sound feel alive. The human ear identified with it. It could excite and uplift or release emotions of suffering. Average musicians seemed not to understand about energy or could not manage it. It was a technique you might learn, but to do it well you needed a natural affinity. The energy needed to be dispersed as if telling a story with moments of high and low intensity. Nick had explained this to Julian earlier. She could relate to that and found it interesting.

'What's it like, being a musician?' she asked, while they were amiably looking out over the hill behind the pub.

'You don't mean how well it pays, I presume,' Nick grinned.

'No, of course not,' Julian smiled back.

'I can only speak for myself. It's my way of living.'

Nick gave it some thought. Julian waited.

'Like all art, it isn't an easy way. Many give up because of circumstances. Or frustration from lack of success. Not getting to where you feel you could be.'

'It's a lonely road,' Julian suggested.

'Possibly. It's also fascinating, if you are wired in that way.'

'But you pay a price?'

'Yes. For all art there is always a price to pay. It can be exhausting work with lots of practice. For some that may deliver handsomely. I'm lucky to be one of those, simply because of Tom.' Nick had no illusions about that. 'You need luck in this industry, and persistence.'

'But you must be very good, Nick. Tom never settles for second best.'

'I suppose,' Nick had to admit. 'There are many good musicians though who will remain forever unknown.'

'Is there a deeper dynamic to being a real musician than ability and hard work?' Julian asked. Her interest in psycho-spirituality raised that question.

'I think so. You must have music in your bones. You need to get it, though that is an obscure statement,' Nick replied. 'Music is an intuitive language. Also, a feel for the instruments you play is essential.'

'Which would be a few different ones. If you're a real musician,' Julian assumed.

'Yes. But usually one or two are your best.'

Nick refrained from mentioning his, though bass obviously was one of them. Instead he asked what made someone a special education teacher.

Julian thought that over. She might have expected the question. Nick was in no hurry to get his answer and lazily gazed around. Julian had an idea.

'It's like reading a musical score,' she explained.

That got his attention.

'Most people can read other people okay. Reading an ordinary behavioural score is not overly complicated. It's amazing how quickly many folk still make a mess of it.'

Julian felt her explanation was taking shape.

'Some behavioural scores are hard to read though. Only those trained for it might manage. A difficult score can be beautiful. But it may seem repulsive unless you are able to discern its beauty.'

'Like modern disjointed classical music. Or jazz for that matter, full of discords,' Nick suggested.

'Yes, like that,' Julian agreed, grateful for his input.

'But you like that kind of music and can read the score?' Nick said.

'I do. There are three kinds of people with regard to

behaviour and intellectual disability.' Julian pressed on.

'Many professionals can read the score, may find it interesting, but don't really like the music.'

'You mean psychologists and the like?' Nick asked.

'Yes, can be. Others like the music, but are not that good at reading the score. Special education teachers may fall into that category. They are good at their job but getting to grips with the individual inner score of each pupil well may be beyond them.'

'Like the competent musician, who just lacks the necessary intuition to be great,' Nick said.

'Like that. The third person likes the music and in with sufficient experience often can read the score. They figure out what is going on in the mind of an intellectually disabled child.'

'And, that's you.' Nick concluded.

'I think so,' Julian had to admit. Experience had born that out. 'Every person has a behavioural score. The children I teach simply have a difficult one. As people they live by a different tune.'

Nick looked at her in admiration. That was nicely explained.

'But there is a fourth person,' Julian decided. 'Those, who don't like the music, have an aversion to the score, but the music falls into their laps anyway. Some parents with a disabled child fall into that category. They are very discontent with what is happening to them. It's sad.'

'You're special, Georgia,' Nick told her. 'I don't think I could succeed in the music you are playing.'

Julian smiled. 'You might surprise yourself, Nick.'

Walking down the street to the car both felt at ease.

***

That evening, after a barbecue, Aluka excused herself for a bath and a book in bed. Three days of musical intensity had worn her out. Tom disappeared into a room where he kept his laptop. To reach overseas contacts who were still in the middle of their working day. Julian and Nick sat lazily on the deck in a perfect night with not a hint of a breeze. Neither of them felt like talking until Nick posed a surprising question. He was in a melancholic mood sipping his second whiskey. Julian was not sure of her own feelings apart from them being kind of sad but not unhappy.

'Have you ever been in love, Georgia?' Nick asked with a soft voice. He looked away into the darkness.

It startled Julian. She was unsure how to reply.

Nick had not expected an answer and he continued.

'We've talked about visions lately,' he said. 'I had one not that long ago while listening to a track of jazz music.'

Julian remained silent. She understood that no reply was expected to what Nick was to say.

'You know what I saw? An enormous movement of love behind the pain in the world, or at least behind my pain. It blew me away.'

He sipped his whiskey. Kept looking out over the balustrade, but not focusing.

'You know what that pain asked me? "For how long will you fight me?"'

Nick stopped talking taken up with thoughts far away. Julian made sure not to disrupt the quiet.

'I understood that the way in which to defeat pain is to try and roll with it. I also knew the real reason for my pain – I had loved someone. Love and pain seem to go together. If I believe what you told me, and I do, one day only love will remain.'

Julian sat in her chair not knowing how to respond. She began to feel Nick's pain. Her mind refused to think anything. Any thought was bound to be inadequate right now.

'You know, Georgia. I have tried hard to roll with the punches, but it can be ever so difficult. It's getting better. Sometimes though, it's not. Love can hurt you, Georgia, like nothing else can.'

'Oh, Nick,' she said spontaneously.

It made him turn towards her briefly. She saw the struggle etched on his face.

'You know what Helen's last words were to me?' he commented. 'She said, "Oh, Nick," just like you.'

Julian felt as if she had been hit. Told herself to keep it together.

'Helen then said, "Don't have me worry about you, hey?"' Nick swallowed hard resting back in his easy chair.

'I'm trying to achieve that, Georgia. But it can be so difficult. Love is a hard taskmaster.'

Nick had closed his eyes now. He had finished. Julian said not a word. Her heart was in absolute turmoil.

'Sorry, Georgia,' Nick mumbled. 'You deserve better from me. It's such a mess at times.'

Slowly Julian got up. Nick was out of reach and not because of alcohol, but of grief. These were not the ramblings of an inebriated man but of one who was hurting much. Quietly, she left him for her bedroom sensing that Nick didn't notice. He seemed completely oblivious to everything and perhaps had fallen asleep.

Julian sat down on her bed feeling gutted. Not ever had she been confronted with pain like that. Her heart was racing. She told herself to take deep breaths and calm down. Nick would be okay. It was not as if grief was new to him. He had lived with it and was a survivor. The few days she had known him made that clear. Perhaps Julian taking her into his confidence involved a healing dynamic. He would never have spoken of his feelings like that to just anyone. First the book and now this, Julian thought. At least there seemed to be chemistry between them that made him opening up possible. It is what you would be hoping for when falling in love. That you are found attractive and considered worthy of confidences. All the same, Julian felt gutted. Her mind was in a muddle.

She tried to pray, but to no avail. The daily office, which, she had attempted to follow faithfully during her holidays, was of no help right now. The words didn't seem relevant. Which was nonsense, of course. Still, now wasn't a time for talking to God. She would just sit in reflection with her thoughts. God could read those perfectly.

Nick's vision had been about suffering love. Those two words were wonderfully descriptive, but of little help when you had to live it through. And it would be glib to suggest that all shall be well. Even though that was true eternally. With Nick, it would be a platitude right now, Julian concluded. So, what to do? There was nothing she could do but love Nick. Though he had no idea about her feelings. She could pray and would. Nick, himself, he had to wrestle with his plight. Fortunately, he felt not sorry for himself and had good people nearby. Like his neighbours and Tom. Matters would improve over time. Nick had indicated that to be so already. Love can hurt you, Georgia. Those words of Nick were so true.

Why people had to hurt so greatly, whatever the reason,

that question Julian felt powerless about. Theological answers came up way short in satisfying the everyday person. For theology to be of help you needed faith. You could invite people into faith but never impose it. There wasn't a non-religious answer to suffering. Even then, the answer was of little practical help. And yet it was a help. Nick was capable of faith which gave Julian some comfort. Oh Nick, she groaned making ready for bed.

19

NICK WAS TEN MINUTES AWAY from collecting Nutty. He felt exhausted and raw. Georgia had been incredible this morning after his downer last night. Nick could kick himself for what he perceived to have been insensitive and selfish behaviour. His attempt to explain it had been cut off with a smile and a peck on his cheek. Just leave it, Nick, she had said, you're okay. However, he did not feel like leaving it and did he feel okay. Something about him had to change.

They had flown out from Ballina, a short drive south of Lennox Head. In Melbourne he had thanked Tom and Aluka for taking good care of him. His goodbye to Georgia had been reserved, as if they both avoided spontaneity. Georgia's eyes had shone a little, when she suggested he might come and visit her. He had been feeling so flat in that airport, that his response hardly exceeded the non-committal. Don't make such an ass of yourself, Nick had chided himself. But he could not muster the energy to sound enthusiastic. A dull depression had settled upon him that morning. It was impossible to shake off.

George and Mandy's farm came in sight. Upon arrival he found Nutty running around waiting – wildly excited. She would have recognised the sound of his car from afar. Nick let the dog climb all over him and ruffled her for a long time. Mandy stood at the door and invited him in. She noticed that today Nick was not a well man. She sat him down at the kitchen table with his usual coffee. So sensitive, she thought, and so much struggle. What might have happened?

Nick felt quite at home here now and needed not pretend. Charles and Mandy were aware of his history. They had taken to him for which Nick was grateful. After a while of sitting opposite each other, with Nick staring into his drink, Mandy took the bull by the horns.

'Has Georgia hurt you, Nick?' It was a possibility.

He looked up confused, as if getting used to that idea.

'Heavens no,' he said. 'I have hurt her.'

'What happened?' Mandy asked kindly.

Nick explained. How he felt that he had been quite insensitive throwing far too much into her lap. All of that while she was on her holidays. She had been terrific and deserved much better. He had failed her.

Mandy gave that some thought. How to best help Nick. She decided not to beat about the bush.

'Had it occurred to you that Georgia might be in love with you, Nick?' Mandy asked. 'To me it looked a real possibility.'

That comment made him sit up straight. He looked perplexed.

'I figure,' Mandy continued, 'that she decided the time of you being together to be too short to let on. Also, she knows of your hurt and needs to be sure that indeed she loves you and is not leading you up the garden path.'

Mandy had thought of Georgia and with female intuition was convinced that cupid had struck firmly. Of course, you could never know how that was to develop. With her back in England, not being on holidays, and ordinary life taking over. Still, Mandy was hopeful.

Depression tends to make people unreceptive to future possibilities and with Nick it was no different. He was gazing at the table again, slightly sideways. What Mandy had just told him, if he was even to believe it, fully confirmed that he had mucked things up properly.

'Listen, Nick,' Mandy said firmly. 'I'd like to tell you something.'

She waited for him to look up.

'I have a good idea what life has dealt you. I realise, those blows always attack a person's vulnerabilities. It can lead to addictions and surely depression. Defences against hurt go up as well. It all seems normal to me. But the most dangerous defence of them all, the one you should avoid like a plague, is to be afraid to love once more, because you might get hurt again. You should never allow that defence to happen.'

Nick sat back in his chair and looked at the ceiling. He would rather not be hearing this. The problem was obvious and thus far he had not acknowledged it to be true to his situation. He looked at Mandy.

She saw a man with tired eyes who needed a break from everything. But she could not offer him that. Her woman's heart skipped a beat. It will work out, she told herself.

'Years ago I read a book that quoted the first line of the novel *Fortitude* written by Hugh Walpole,' Mandy continued. 'You know what it said?' She waited till Nick looked at her. 'It said, '"Tisn't life that counts; it's the courage you bring to it." I have never forgotten that Nick and held on to it many a time.'

'It's not life that counts, but the courage you bring to it,' Nick repeated, sort of involuntarily. It was a good sentence.

'Yes,' Mandy said. 'Give that some thought. You're made of stuff stern enough to make it count.'

'Thanks, Mandy.' Nick stood up from the table. 'You're a treasure.'

So are you my man, Mandy thought. She would have gladly given him a hug, but refrained from it.

Back at the old dairy Nick looked at Helen's picture as if asking for some help. None was forthcoming, of course.

Once again he promised her she need not worry about him. All he needed now was a good sleep. That Georgia might be in love with him he could hardly believe. Nothing she had done gave any sign of it. But then, perhaps it had. The manner in which she had cared and taken all he had thrown at her without a moment's complaint; it could well be a display of love. I'm just a blind male, Nick thought, engrossed in his pities. What really did he know about women? Perhaps that was his depression talking. He decided to hit the sack without a drink though he craved one badly. He needed to show at least some control over his life right now. Not having a whiskey was a step forward. Never having one again, that was too much to ask.

Nick saw the text on the wall by Julian of Norwich: *Alle Shalle Be Wele*. He took it down and stuck it into the bottom of the dresser. Too many memories of Helen and now Georgia from that text. He simply didn't wish to be reminded of that every time he sat in his kitchen during the months ahead. Now he was missing two women who had become dear to him. One had left him forever, the other he had never held close and might not ever do. Tomorrow he would take the chainsaw to the trees and make a mighty racket, work himself into a sweat. Nutty would have a ball.

***

Julian sat slumped sideways in her seat looking out of the window at the clouds below. That afternoon she had spent at Tom and Aluka's with time moving along too quickly. Her holidays were at an end. The answer she was looking for had become clear. Whether Nick and she would ever get together had no bearing on that. Tom had asked about Nick and she had told him. He had understood. Musicians tended to be a sensitive breed and with the added troubles of grief life could be misery. Tom had encouraged her not to worry. Nick was a survivor and he would keep an eye on him. It was a comforting thought. Saying goodbye at the airport Nick had looked terrible. She had almost said, 'Oh, Nick,' again and embraced him. An impulse that she had checked just in time.

Julian felt a bit powerless. There was little she could do to support Nick soon being on the other side of the world. They did not actually have a relationship beyond being friends. The wisdom of that was not in doubt. She would just have to get through the next three months and see whether Nick would arrive in Liverpool after his gig in London. The booking of *M-Jazz Indigo* in a club in Soho was basically a certainty, Tom had told her.

Last night, she had fallen into a deep sleep with an ache

in her heart. She had pondered about being thrown into the deep end. From the sheltered existence of a religious sister, she had come to see the hurts of a man she was falling in love with. All within days. The complexities of life quickly were staring her in the face. And as strange as it might seem, it was the beginning of her liberation. An unkind word to use, for she had always been free, really. Her community had its rules, but nothing overly restrictive. She lived in a caring environment. In truth, this perception of being hemmed in had arisen since arriving in Australia. Still, it felt as if part of her sought to break out. Such a frustration always needed careful handling. Feelings could run deep. They were unreasonable by nature, and might respond with force when stirred. Once they cut loose, you could be in for a surprise, for better or worse. With her they had cut loose for the better this morning.

She had taken a hot shower to wash stress and tension away. She had lifted her face full-on into the spray and spontaneously took a long time massaging her body all over, like she had not done for almost a decade. After a hard rub with the towel drying off, her skin buffeted into a glow, she had stood up tall, pulled her shoulders back and looked into the mirror. Everything looked good. All was firm. Words from the Song of Solomon had come to mind: 'Behold you are beautiful my love, behold, you are beautiful.' She no longer felt like a nun. Her body was there to be used. It should be used. She had stood for well over a minute in touch with her feelings and experienced vibrancy not previously hers. Desire had enveloped her like a cloak. She had let it settle, brought it under firm control as she knew she could. The power of womanhood had been hers for the taking and with her whole being she had taken it. It had been an unexpected and incredible experience of body awareness. There was no point in denying that. The human person was wonderfully made.

She had sensed the presence of goodness and holiness in that bathroom. She would never be able to describe what that feeling had really been like. It had taken her ages to dress and come down to a sense of normality. One thing now was crystal clear. She would be a woman who might bear children. That was the message. Being a religious sister was an honourable vocation, never to be ridiculed. She did not in the least regret ever making that choice. But soon she would be Georgia again. And Nick would always be so wonderfully Nick, she mused with a smile.

The old dairy came to mind, and while thinking of Nutty, sleep caught up with her in a plane was moving smoothly towards London at over 500 miles per hour.

PART THREE

20

M-JAZZ INDIGO was into its third and final set in a club in London. Nick had Georgia on his mind. He saw the lady he had spoken to during the break make her way to the back of the dimly lit hall. He felt for her and her loneliness. The band was playing *The Girl from Ipanema*, which was one of his favourites. He liked the Latin American beat which Jeremy was able to maintain while giving it some grunge. It was not quite jazz/metal they were playing now. Their sound had an edge with Aluka's voice coming out above it as smooth as silk. She was a real jazz singer at heart, Nick concluded, once again. *M-Jazz Indigo* had a future. The crowd seemed to get it. Not only that, they enjoyed he music. As expected, Vorque was the main attraction. But the audience knew they were listening to a set of fine musicians overall.

They had played at pubs in Melbourne and Sydney to get performances under their belt. It had stirred publicity in the grapevine, some radio play and interviews. With a promise that soon they would be back. Tom though would not muddle about small-time. His stature as a musician allowed exposure in notable places. The biggest markets were in Europe and the USA where he was well-known. Their performances would be mainly overseas. That was fine by Nick, though he didn't really like travelling. But he enjoyed being on a stage. Pumping nice lines out of the bass felt like being extended into the ether. For the audience to connect with. Music needed sharing to fulfil its destiny. It was the wish of every musician. He had been in the zone during the previous set. Not quite so this time. Still, the guitar, piano, drum and bass gelled beautifully.

Nick had Georgia on his mind for good reasons. It was the last gig of *M-Jazz Indigo* in London. The coming weekend they would play in Berlin, starting Saturday. That left him a few days to make his way to Liverpool. He forced himself to concentrate on the music. Half an hour and the set would be done.

While packing up their instruments Tom asked Nick to give his regards to his sister. With a grin he suggested Nick should take firm hold of the lass. For they deserved each other. Nick smiled sheepishly. That may be true, but he felt no certainty. It reminded him of Mandy. She had asked whether he would visit Georgia once in England. His affirmative answer had pleased her. Now, don't be a fool Nick, Mandy had warned him. You are worthy of her. All you have to do is open your arms wholeheartedly.

Forget kicking yourself. That's what it's about, good relationships. Coming to grips with each other's history and peculiarities. You've done no wrong. Take courage. And give Georgia my best wishes.

Mandy had been right, of course. That idea about facing life with courage had been helpful. Obviously, his friends saw something he could still only hope for. Try as he might, doubts kept nagging at him.

Back at his hotel he enjoyed a whiskey before trying to sleep. He let Georgia rumble through his thoughts. His head was buzzing, as invariably it did after a performance. Soon, he would meet her again. He could hardly wait. Since she had flown away three months ago life had trundled on as usual. His depression had eased. Nutty, the old dairy and his music, had kept him engaged. Depression could hit without notice at any time. But if he remained positive, life was manageable.

He had not been in contact with Georgia. Apart from an email of late arranging their meeting up. Staying in touch with anyone was not one of his strengths. With the situation between them in kind of limbo, it felt as if seeing her again was needed before regular communications. Most likely that was a cop-out but Nick had known of being in England soon. Georgia had concluded likewise, it seemed. She had made no contact apart from thanking him for a good time once back in

England. He had felt that depressed and guilty about his behaviour that she never got much of a reply. Just him wishing her the best in the fewest of words. So where that left him now, he was unsure about. Confidence with women was not him, Nick knew. Helen had virtually dragged him into their relationship. She had not needed to pull very hard though. Dawn was near. His train departed midday, so that left a few hours for a sleep

***.

Georgia Ketteling was waiting in a café at the station feeling nervous. Nick would soon arrive and she had been counting the days. She had been not quite sure whether he would come and visit her while in England. Regardless of Tom considering it a no-brainer. Nick's email had been wonderful news. Tom had told her that Nick was okay, but uncertain about her view of him. Not that it was ever discussed. It's just the kind of guy he is, Tom had said. You will have to take charge, Sis.

Georgia was willing to do so. She would take the first step, if needed, and let Nick respond. Not ever would she wish to become the dominant female. Her heart was in a flutter. Julian of Norwich spoke of Jesus' thirst for his people.[69] That was a fine way of describing how she felt. She still remembered her last look at Nick vividly. The drawn face and tired eyes. At that airport in

Melbourne. A photo she had taken of him and Nutty during her holidays stood on a tallboy in her room. He had looked happy that time. She had prayed for Nick every day. Right now, she was trying to convince herself that she had no idea how seeing him again might affect her. Apart from feeling quite excited about it. That thought was delusional. She knew that she had much stronger emotions. They would need to be kept in check.

Much had happened since her holiday in Australia. She had left the order with a blessing and found herself a small bedsit with a tiny but adequate kitchen. Her last evening at the community had been a teary affair. Everyone was kind and understanding and said she would be badly missed. That had been precious. Being a qualified special education teacher, someone with a profession, enabled her to keep her job. The staff took their time in calling her Georgia instead of Julian. They still were not quite used to it. One staff member felt as if Julian now was to become another person to her. Georgia herself had felt odd about the name change as well, but not for long. Sister Julian was no more. A memory of the past. The Lord had been kind in showing her that so clearly. She had never doubted her decision not to renew her vows to be the right one.

Cooking a meal for one person only and not for group of sisters at first had been strange. Shopping for one and paying bills, it all highlighted how different her life had become. Doing as you please and when you please had been a nice new experience. Living all by yourself in small rooms was cosy, but lonely. She had come to appreciate how hard it must be for Nick on that large property. That would soon change, if she had any say in it. But she should not get ahead of herself. She wondered what Nick would be like when in a few minutes they would set eyes on each other. It was easy for Tom to suggest that she grab hold of him, as he called it. He was not the one facing the situation. Nick needed respect and she would make sure that he received just that.

Georgia had asked for permission at work to leave early. All this morning it had been difficult to concentrate on her job. Lindy, who helped in the classroom every day, had given her an inquiring look. They were good friends. The train was to arrive within minutes. It was time to walk to the platform. Georgia felt slightly lightheaded, with a twirl in her stomach.

The passengers spilled out of each carriage like ants on a mission. Most knew exactly where they were headed but for a few to whom the station was unknown. One of those was Nick. When the foot traffic eased Georgia noticed him immediately in the distance at the second to last carriage. He waved to her and she began walking. Her steps became increasingly fast. When just meters from Nick she found herself almost at a run. He opened his arms wide, caught her, lifted her up, and swung her from side to side. Neither of them could speak. After a while Nick eased her slowly to the ground.

'Oh, Nick,' Georgia groaned into his shoulder.

He stroked her hair not saying a word. He just did not wish to let go.

'Come, let me show you Liverpool,' Georgia said at last gruffly disentangling herself from his embrace.

Nick smiled broadly. 'You bet,' he agreed.

Hand in hand they walked out of the station.

To Nick Liverpool was like all major cities – busy and in a hurry. He was bound to visit a few of those in his musical career. Georgia suggested they would find a place to sit down and chat. She looked radiant, Nick thought, so very happy. He felt wonderful himself. All his doubts had evaporated the moment he had caught her at the railway station. It was incredible. Something had taken over and oh my, oh boy. He was unaware that Georgia was silently thanking the Lord. She had no doubt that he had pulled a few heavenly strings at that moment cutting through all questions and reservations like a knife through butter. They walked into a pub with a view of the River Mersey in the distance. Nick settled on a beer and Georgia ordered a cider.

'So much I'd like to know, Nick,' she said once they were seated.

'Fire away,' Nick replied amused. It was just like Helen, always asking about what was happening. And he felt no guilt about that thought. As if being close to another woman, such a fabulous one, would dishonour his first love. His mind registered this and quietly he gave thanks. Helen would hang around, but supportively so.

'How's Nutty?'

'Pining away for your company, Georgia,' Nick responded and checked himself. Georgia was genuinely interested in his kelpie, which was great. 'She's doing as well as ever,' he added.

Georgia looked at Nick. It was good news that he felt like a bit of banter. She had not got that from him before.

'How's Mandy?'

'Trying to convince me that you love me.' It was true enough.

'She saw it right away, you know,' Georgia solicited.

''Yes,' Nick had to agree. 'She suggested the idea to me the day you flew off. I thought it a fantasy.'

'When you were helping Charles in the shed, she told me not to lead you on unless I was serious. I was not to hurt you.'

That information surprised Nick. He hadn't known.

'Wonderful, don't you think?' Georgia suggested.

'Mandy and Tom seemed to know a lot more than I.'

'Yes, they did,' Georgia confirmed deciding not to mention that Tom had also questioned her.

'You're just gorgeous, Georgia,' Nick commented looking at her with great affection.

'The kind of person you would do anything for?'

Nick looked nonplussed. Something about the question jarred. It did not seem like the Georgia he thought he knew.

'I'm having you on, Nick,' Georgia said with a smile. 'I promise never to be manipulative. But I have a request that is important to me.'

'Out with it,' Nick suggested.

'I would like you to see where I work. Tomorrow, after lunch, there is a concert at school performed by the students, well some of them. I would like you to attend.'

That was one out of left field for Nick. It took him a moment to take it in. The request was reasonable enough and he remembered the pub at Bangalow. Their discussion about Georgia's profession. He should get to know about her job first hand. It was a good idea.

'Do I have to purchase a ticket for the show?' Nick asked considering it unlikely. His question confirmed his willingness to show up.

'I'm your ticket, Nick,' Georgia said with a grin. 'That should be ample.'

21

NICK ARRIVED AT THE FRONT GATE of Talitha
Cumi Special School having no idea what to expect.
Georgia's invitation had been fair enough. The least he
could do was to see what her work entailed. Like most
others, he had seen people with an intellectual disability.
But had never actually related to them socially. At a party
once he had the opportunity, but avoided it. Those who
interacted with the disabled understood people in a way
foreign to him, Nick had concluded that night. Now, he
was in love with such a person. He would be receptive to
the environment he was about to enter.

A friendly woman at the gate welcomed the guests for
that afternoon. The concert was for parents and care
givers. Even the press had been invited. It was lunchtime
with the yard full of children. Georgia must have kept an
eye out and soon appeared. She had a mischievous little
smile. He grinned manfully.

Only a few meters through the gate and he was
arrested by a tall lanky boy with a slightly unbalanced gait.
He came up close and stared Nick brazenly into the face.

'Who are you?' he asked. 'Who are you?' There was no sense of real interest or emotion behind the question.

Georgia said nothing leaving Nick to deal with it.

'I'm Nick,' said Nick putting on a smile and looking straight back.

'Nick,' he said. 'Nick.' He turned and walked away having satisfied his curiosity about this stranger.

'Come on,' Georgia said. 'I will have to sign you in at reception and quickly show you around. Then I'll leave you and get my class ready for the concert.'

There was everything as might be expected. The school featured a large variety of play equipment outside in the grounds, plus an art and music room, a kitchen and computer room, many class rooms and the gym where the concert would take place. When he entered Georgia's class room Nick wondered how you could spent most of your day there with unintentionally challenging children. He would walk out screaming before the passing of an hour, he silently confessed. The room was not very large.

'How many children do you teach here?' Nick asked.

'Six. Together with Lindy my education support officer,' Georgia replied. She gave him an enquiring look.

'What?' Nick asked. 'You're incredible.' Perhaps that was what he was meant to say.

Georgia grinned. 'I've got another request,' she said.

Here we go, Nick thought, wondering.

'It will be my last one. I promise.'

'Till when?'

'For a long time.' Georgia looked at him in a way that crumbled all his defences.

How could I ever deny her anything, Nick thought humorously? Oh, this Georgia.

'Would you play a song for us at the concert, at the end?'

This threw Nick for a moment.

'I've got no guitar.' It was a feeble objection, for obviously Georgia would be aware of that. The question of performing was settled in the way a salesman begins to fill out the order without ever asking whether the client actually wishes to buy the car.

'Our music teacher has one that we can borrow,' Georgia explained. 'Let's go and get it. I have permission for all of this. Those in the know are looking forward to your contribution.'

'I will need to tune it first,' Nick explained. He had a number of ways in which to tune a guitar and it was unlikely that the one on offer would be at his preferred setting.

The instrument was a good one. Georgia left Nick in a small room to tune up and walked back to her classroom. Though apprehensive, Nick felt okay. He suspected that Georgia wished for him to be exposed to an experience that was to change his view on special education and intellectually disabled children. What that would mean, he had no idea about. When, as directed, he walked into the back of the gym, it seemed pandemonium. Joel the music teacher met him with the suggestion that the guitar be kept near the front and out of reach of the children. Nick would receive it back, connected to an amp, once he was ready to go.

The hall was a playground at lunchtime every day. Today though, it needed to be vacated early because of the concert. Teachers and assistants were trying as calmly as possible to encourage a number of students to leave the equipment earlier than usual, but were not understood. Objections and reluctance was noticeable everywhere. A change of routine upset the children inordinately. Nick took a deep breath taking it in. This would be some show to come.

Much of the school would attend. Children with a developmental age of two and three, who were in fact much older in years, were excluded. The event, loud and with a crowd, would be beyond what they could cope with. Soon students began to arrive with their teachers. The noise was incredible and the excitement great. Staff was patiently responding to the challenge of this once-a-year event. Their student's reactions differed from those of normal days when their routines were predictable. Making sure pupils were seated sort of orderly was a major task. Quiet persistence seemed to be the key. The students who were to perform were at the back. Nick sat at the outer edge midway with other visitors.

The concert began. Every class made a contribution. Staff unsure how things would turn out. Usually, nothing went quite to plan. There was the unexpected by some and the lack of performance by others. When children were acting, it was without self-consciousness. The singing could be surprisingly pitch-perfect. A departure from the script was sometimes obvious, a meltdown possible, and always there was the laughter. Everyone had a ball. It was impossible to be critical. To Nick the show was a wonder of joy and celebration. He was beginning to see the funny side. Also the great work of the staff in orchestrating an event that belonged to the curriculum of any school – a concert.

The main act, as always, came last. There was a buzz in the air. The work experience group of 15-16 year olds was to perform. They attended a sheltered workshop once a week learning to work in teams while packaging screws for hardware stores or headphones for local airlines. They got used to following and complete their allocated tasks. If able to work independently, a job and money would be a possibility in future.

This senior group now walked up from the back. Their props were in place including a car made up out of cardboard during their art lessons. It was bright red and had been painstakingly constructed. The last act of the day came from *Grease*. It was Lenny's idea, who thus qualified as the main performer. Everyone waited in anticipation. Nick wondered what was to happen. How much of a show the group would be able to put on. After the first loud notes of *Greased Lightning* the school was beginning to rock and roll. The fast 4/4 beat of the music filled the hall. The seniors danced like movie stars. Some really sang along with the soundtrack while others mimed as if their lives depended on it. Being out of sync, it mattered not. The original script, with the girl Sandy from the movie also dancing along in the scene, was partly ignored. Lenny made all the moves and some more. The visitors were soon clapping along moving rhythmically in their seats. 'Go Greased Lightning, go, go, go ……..' In the end pandemonium broke loose. Nick had not had so much fun for a long time. The seniors received a rapturous applause before making their way to their seats, proud as punch.

Oh, dear, Nick thought. Georgia was walking up to the microphone. She announced that they had a visitor in their midst who was a professional musician of note. He had declared his willingness to perform in ending the concert. Let's give Nick a clap. Joel was waiting with the guitar and Nick approached the microphone. He took a few seconds to fine-tune the instrument. The strings of a guitar would adjust to room temperature and the hall now was hot. After acknowledging that he could simply never live up to the previous performance, he announced that his song would be known to everyone and they should sing along as loudly as they felt to. While people were wondering, Nick began with an intro. Immediately you could hear a bass line, chords and melody notes in one with a distinct rhythm, all effortlessly smooth and tight. Georgia was mesmerised and not the only one. She had never heard Nick play and now understood how gifted he was.

After the first words of the lyrics, 'I've paid my dues, time after time,' Lenny rushed from the back taking the second microphone next to Nick. He had recognised the song immediately. *We are the Champions* by Queen. Lenny was musical and had a good voice. Soon the hall was swinging along singing, 'We are the champions, my friends. We'll keep on fighting till the end.' Lenny became Freddie Mercury personified making giant steps with the mike close to his mouth, one arm straight up high into the air, and looking sideways at the audience. Nick stopped singing and left the show to the new superstar. Joel cranked up the amplifier for the guitar not to be drowned out by the noise. 'No time for losers, 'cause we are the champions – of the world!' Everybody was joining in. Nick had performed in a lot of places, but would never forget this one. Silently he thanked Georgia for this opportunity. Everyone applauded with gusto.

'Can you play, *You never walk alone?*' Lenny asked keeping the microphone to his chest. The audience could hear the question clearly. A few shouts of yes and more could be heard, also from the students. Nick had played it once at a friend's wedding years ago. As a true musician he did not often forget a song, but was uncertain about the words.

'You sing it Lenny, and I will follow,' he said. 'Just give me a minute to find the right key.' Nick was cottoning on fast. If he were to strike the wrong chord first, Lenny might take off like a rocket and leave everyone high and dry. Lenny understood and was waiting in anticipation. A girl walked up from the back. She would also be a part of this. Her voice was not quite accurate, Nick soon found out, but who cared. The crowd took over anyway.

'When you walk, through the storm,' Lenny began with the audience joining in almost immediately, 'hold your head up high, and don't be afraid of the dark.' Soon the hall was singing full on once more. 'Walk on, walk on, you'll never walk alone.' If ever Nick had enjoyed a great celebration, this was one. Everyone was happy and at the end applauded, with Nick pointing to Lenny and the girl as stars of the show. When he gave the guitar back to Joel, he felt moved in his spirit and humbled. Creativity was no respecter of person. It had been a fine time.

Nick had a brief chat with some auxiliary staff while the teachers and assistants were busy guiding the pupils back to their classrooms. Visitors also expressed their thanks. The principal of the school looked at him with kind intelligent eyes and was smiling warmly. She seemed to have come to a conclusion that remained unspoken. Nick vaguely noticed this and sort of wondered. Georgia soon appeared not uttering a word about the show though her eyes said it all. She needed to be back in class and help the children onto the school bus for the next hour. Could Nick keep himself busy and be at the gate by then? Nick took a walk through the street to clear his head from that great concert.

'Now, I understand,' Lindy said. They were clearing up at the end of the day.

'What?'

'Why all those changes of late. You're in love.' She gave Georgia a speculative look.

Georgia smiled at her happily.

'Not bad for a nun,' Lindy grinned.

'Nun no more, Lindy.'

'No, obviously not. I would change my nationality to score a bloke like that.'

'Perhaps, I will.' Georgia looked at her best friend

with a glint in her eyes

'I see. He's Australian, isn't he? I thought I heard an accent.'

'With a dog called Nutty and a farm,' Georgia said.

'And you're nutty about that too.'

'About everything, Lindy. About everything.'

Lindy saw the delight on her co-worker's face. They had taught together for years. When the day came for Georgia to leave, she would miss her badly.

'Good on you, girl,' she said giving it the thumbs up. 'You deserve every bit of it. Give me a hug.'

The two women embraced.

'Don't be so stupid as to let him slip through your fingers,' Lindy admonished with a tear in her eyes.

'As if I would,' Georgia replied. She had not felt that free and happy in all her life.

22

GEORGIA LOCKED ARMS WITH NICK, squeezed hard and said, 'I feel like a cup of soup and know just the place for that.' They walked around the corner not far to her favourite eatery. Much personal reflection had busied her in that place over time. It had been her bolt-hole from school and vocation. The soup of the day was always nice. It was just what she felt like to complete her afternoon of triumph. For that was how she viewed what had taken place. Not the triumph of having conquered, but one of jubilation. What she had hoped for, and in fact expected, had happened and beyond. Nick was fabulous. The more she knew him, the better it became. Would you be so lucky? She was no fan of Kylie Minogue, but that little lyric was spot on.

Nick was only too happy to be guided to a cup of soup somewhere. He could do with a bit of sustenance. This afternoon had taken it out of him. He felt very satisfied though. Not with his own performance, he was used to that being on par, but with what Georgia had thrown at him. It had been an eye opener. A good and necessary one. His life had been enriched. With more cream on the cake than he had ever hoped for. He was holding on to that cream presently hanging on his arm as if never to let go.

They found a corner table in a cosy and cluttered space with a homely atmosphere. Nick figured it to have been an eating place for many years. It had that feel to it. The soup today was beef vegetable with a chunk of freshly baked bread and butter. When the waitress placed their meals before them she asked how Julian was keeping. Georgia noticed Nick's face becoming confused. It would have been impossible to tell everyone of her change of name and the reason for it. In places she had remained Julian.

'What's this Julian?' Nick asked. 'One of the children at school called you that, but I thought it was because of her disability. That she was confusing you with someone else.'

Georgia looked at him intently. 'Hold on to your seat, Nick.'

'Okay, I will,' Nick said, beginning to spoon his soup. It tasted excellent. He wondered where this was leading. Georgia's suggestion of holding on made him expect it to be surprising. But never would he have imagined what he was to hear.

'I used to be known as Julian before when living as a religious sister. I was a nun.'

Nick's spoon stopped mid-air in making its way to his mouth, spilling soup on the table. He slowly put the utensil back into the bowl utterly amazed.

'You were a nun?' His ears could hardly believe what he had just said.

'Yes, till only recently.' Georgia smiled. She felt a little sorry for him. What a day. First Nick had been thrown into the deep end at her school and now he was finding out about Julian, the nun. But she saw the funny side and was determined to keep it light hearted.

'What about during your holidays in Australia?'

'I had come over to see Tom and decide whether to remain a nun,' Georgia explained. 'Meeting you made that decision easy.'

'Tom knew about it all, I presume?'

'Yes, of course. He was the only one. He never liked the idea of his little sister being a nun and nothing in the world could have persuaded him to call me Julian. So in Australia I was Georgia, which I expected soon to become again anyway.'

Nick shook his head. He could not help but smile. In a way it was hilarious, him falling in love with a nun.

Georgia noticed it and was relieved. 'So now, you will walk away from me,' she suggested mischievously.

Nick grabbed a piece of bread, ripped a piece off, and stuck it into his mouth. While chewing away he said nothing, just looked at her with humorous eyes. He could have made any kind of comment about nuns and had a few ready. But it would not be funny. Georgia had taken her vocation seriously and he would never sully that. They locked eyes for a moment. If love was a glint, they both saw it.

'Why Julian for a name?' Nick asked. It must be that book perhaps.

Georgia hesitated and made up her mind. She would never to be in competition with Helen or avoid mentioning her. They would have had a lot in common, she imagined.

'Basically, because of a book. The same book Helen was reading.'

This reference to Helen gave Nick a faint check in his spirit. He was pleased about its mildness.

'I felt called to become a religious sister while in the Norwich Cathedral, during my university days,' Georgia continued. 'I had visited the cell of Julian of Norwich elsewhere and later on read her book. It presented me with ideas about my faith that I had never heard before. When taking my vows I could think of no better name change but to Julian.'

Nick nodded his head. That kind of idea would have appealed to Helen, had she ever felt to enter a religious order.

Georgia concentrated on her soup.

'What made you decide to stop being a nun?' Nick

asked the obvious next question.

Her confrontation with the idea of motherhood and its potential loss Georgia had no intention of revealing. Nor would she mention the rediscovering of herself as a woman willingly in touch with her sexual desires. She would keep it simple.

'The time was closing in for me to decide whether to remain a religious sister. That question is asked sort of every three years. Life has its phases and it became clear that my religious vocation phase was coming to an end.'

Nick saw no problem with that. It made perfect sense. When Georgia asked him whether he had ever read the notes she had sent him on *Julian's Windows* and *Agapino* he shook his head negatively. He felt it needed an explanation.

'I could not manage it,' he confessed. 'With Helen and you both out of my life, it simply was too much.'

Georgia was touched. She might have expected this. 'Hey Nick,' she said waiting for him to look up. 'I'm sorry, but I had no option. It all happened too soon.'

'And then I made it worse with our last evening together,' Nick offered.

That needed putting into perspective. Georgia was glad the problem got a mention.

'No, you made it better, Nick,' she said, 'not worse. That you could open up to me as you did proved much of what I was hoping for. I was in love with you and you trusted me with your deepest thoughts. It confirmed that my feelings had a future. There was no way I could tell you that though.'

Nick gazed away over her shoulder letting those words sink in.

'That vision you had of a suffering love, that was incredible,' Georgia continued. 'It aligns exactly with what Julian of Norwich is about and also what Helen would have understood when she was so sick.'

Nick listened carefully.

'Of course, I have never been that ill, but I can well imagine what thoughts might have gone through her mind. She would have experienced Jesus as close. She would have understood that her pain was being born up into the love of God. Eternal goodness and her reward were waiting. More and more she would have drifted towards that promise in her spirit until finally she was allowed to step over the final hurdle into her liberation.'

Georgia stopped, a little taken aback. What had urged her to venture along this path when really all she wished to do was be with Nick and enjoy each other's company?

Nick saw her discomfort. 'Georgia,' he said, 'you're wonderful. Helen no longer has to worry about me.' He felt the significance of that comment deeply. He had tried to live up to that sentence with so much difficulty, and now it would be history.

Georgia reached for his hand across the table and squeezed hard. They sat like that for a while absorbed in their own and each other's feelings.

'You did great today at school, Nick,' Georgia said. 'Lindy, my assistant in class, said she'd kill me if ever I let you slip through my fingers.'

Nick smiled. 'I'll stick to you like glue, Georgia. No slipping will be possible.'

'Thanks, Nick,' she said.

Nick said that he had enjoyed the afternoon though it had been a lot to absorb all in a few hours. Georgia explained how important it had been to her for Nick to be there.

She reflected how for days she had been weighing up whether to ask him. In a way it had been a gamble. Had Nick frozen at the idea, it might have played on her love for him. But she felt she needed to know. She should not have worried.

'You're almost a natural, Nick,' she told him. 'If you get some training.'

'I'm glad, I could read the score a little.' Once again, Nick remembered Bangalow.

'You did fine, Nick'

'When will you have holidays again?' he wondered. Tomorrow, he would be off to Berlin and the thought of being away from Georgia so soon was almost too much to bear. But he had lots of experience in being alone and this time it would be with a big difference.

'I have resigned from my job,' Georgia broke the news. 'I'm coming to Australia.'

'You what?' Nick uttered completely surprised. He had thought about that possibly happening one day, but this was sooner than expected.

'I resigned at the beginning of this term and have four weeks to go.'

'Am I the reason?' Nick asked.

'Yes, of course - and no.'

Georgia explained, that she would have come even if their relationship was not to be. She had taken a shine to the country and wished to be closer to Tom. She felt that a drastic change in her circumstances was needed.

'Of course, mostly, I hoped to come and live with Nutty at the old dairy,' she teased him.

'She'll be so glad to have you, Georgia,' Nick said coming to grips with the good news and thinking of his loyal kelpie friend. 'And so will Mandy.'

'Yes, she told me it would be a pleasure, if ever seeing me back.'

Nick readily believed that and had a thought.

'I'd better pull that text out from the bottom of the dresser.'

'What text is that, Nick?'

'The one I took off the wall when you went back to England. It reminded me too much of one woman I'd lost and of another who was out of reach. Seeing those words every day in my kitchen would have been unbearable.'

'Which words were those, Nick?' Georgia knew full well.

Nick smiled at her sheepishly. He had never really given the promise that much credence. But it had done its work anyway.

Eventually he said, looking Georgia in the eye with great affection,

'Alle Shalle Be Wele'
Julian of Norwich

Thank you for reading *Julian's Windows*.
I hope, you found it interesting.
For more, please see the final pages.
Many blessings,
Michael

Books by Michael J Spyker
Available at agapedeum.com

Trilogy

Meeting Emma

A journey of discovery in which Emma becomes familiar with the many idea of Christian Spirituality through the ages. It helps her towards the person she would like to be. This book has helped many in coming to love the vast wealth of the Christians spiritual tradition.

The Primacy of Love

Jake hears about his father's ideas on God's Love from Baz while travelling the Simpson Desert. Their talks include the significance of eternal and universal love, and the relational. The story has been called a significant theological feat.

The Language of Love

Emma and Jake fall in love. JH introduces them to the real meaning of Eros well beyond merely sex. They learn about being a Friend of Jesus and the language of love. Emma and Jake set off camping in the outback in search of JH. They work out what it means to live intimately together.

Novels

Julian's Windows

A musician and a teacher of children with intellectual ability fall in love. He lost his wife. She questions her vocation as a religious sister. Country life in Victoria restores his soul. A holiday in Australia from Liverpool decides her future. The ideas of Lady Julian of Norwich are an integral part of this love story in a most natural way. Great fun and informative.

Shalomat

Jacq and Ahmed, 16 years old, are on the run through Australia on a quest with mystical dimensions. It draws them together. All seems lost but isn't quite. Young people and adults enjoy this adventure. It is partly a comment on the one-sidedness of modern society and uses ideas of spirituality and philosophy. Will there be a sequel, an appreciative reader asked?

Treatise

Science and Spirit

Science exists by the creativity of God. But where to find God within physics? Where in society, in which God has become irrelevant? An informed answer best includes knowledge of history, science, philosophy, theology and religion. Plus ideas about a way forward. A read of significance to enjoy.

Christian Living

Drawings and Reflections

52 short reflections and 16 drawings that lift the spirit. A brief story that sows an idea. A picture to enjoy. It is not so easy to stay focused in a busy world. A little help always comes in handy. There is nothing religious about this book apart from keeping Jesus in mind and living vibrantly.

References

The references regarding Julian's visions are from
The Classics of Western Spirituality: *Julian of Norwich – Showings*
1978, Paulist Press, New York.
The chapter references concern the Long Text. These chapters
are the same numerically in all publications of the Revelations
(or Showings) and it enables the finding of a reference when
not in possession of the above-mentioned book.

[1] Chapter 5 – p. 184
[2] Chapter 46 – p. 258
[3] Merton, T 2003, *The Inner Experience,* Harper San Francisco, p.
[4] Chapter 4 – p. 181
[5] Chapter 7 – p.p. 188. 189
[6] Chapter 7 – p. 189
[7] Chapter 85 – p. 341
[8] Chapter 52 – p. 280
[9] Luke 1:38
[10] John 2:3
[11] Mark 3:21; 31-34
[12] John 2:3; Mark 3:21 and 31-34
[13] Chapter 7 – p. 187
[14] Chapter 18 – p. 210
[15] Chapter 25 – p. 222
[16] Chapter 57 – p. 292
[17] Chapters 57 - 60
[18] De Chardin, T 1965, *Hymn of the Universe,* Collins, London p. 46
[19] Chapter 63 – p. 305
[20] Chapter 5 – p. 184
[21] Chapter 46 – p. 258
[22] Chapter 56 – p. 288
[23] Chapter 5 – p. 183
[24] Chapter 72 – p. 320
[25] Chapter 71 – p. 318

[26] Chapter 80 – p. 336

[27] Chapter 80 – p. 336

[28] Chapter 77 – p. 331

[29] Chapter 68 – p. 315

[30] Chapter 11 – p. 198

[31] Chapter 27 – p. 225

[32] Chapter 27 – p. 225

[33] Chapter 52 – p. 280

[34] Chapter 21 – p. 215

[35] Chapter 85 – p. 314

[36] Chapter 32 – p. 233

[37] Chapter 32 – p. 232

[38] Chapter 65 – p. 309

[39] Chapter 55

[40] John 1:1-3; Col. 1:15-16; Heb. 1:1-2

[41] Chapters 57 - 60

[42] Chapter 51 – p. 272

[43] Mark 12:25

[44] Chapter 60 – p. 299

[45] Chapter 41 – p. 248

[46] Chapter 31 – p. 230

[47] Chapters 9 – p. 192; 73 – p. 322

[48] Chapters 32 – p. 233; 33 – p. 234

[49] Chapters 68 – p. 314; 70 – p. 317

[50] Chapter 86 – p. 342

[51] Chapter 72 – p. 320

[52] Chapters 4 – p. 181; 77 – p. 331

[53] Chapter 20 – p. 214

[54] Chapter 68 – p. 315

[55] Chapter 74 – p. 324

[56] Chapters 27 – p. 226; 85 – p. 341

[57] Chapter 32 – p. 232

[58] Chapter 33 – p. 234

[59] Chapters 51 – p. 272; 52 – p. 280

[60] Chapter 79 – p. 334

[61] Chapters 27 – p. 226; 50 – p. 266

[62] Chapters 51, 52
[63] Chapter 72 – p. 320
[64] Chapters 46 – p. 259; 49 – p.p. 263, 264
[65] Chapters 39 – p. 245; 58 – p. 294
[66] Chapter 28 – p. 227
[67] Chapter 77 – p. 331
[68] Chapter 72 – p. 72
[69] Chapter 31 – p. 230

"...a **scintillating roman a clef** [and] **salted with witty dialogue**.... I hope he has a sequel up his sleeve."

—JOSEPH DORINSON, PROFESSOR OF HISTORY (RETIRED),
LONG ISLAND UNIVERSITY;
AUTHOR, *JACKIE ROBINSON, RACE, SPORTS
AND THE AMERICAN DREAM*

"**Jim Story is a great storyteller. He has a poet's sensitivity, a historian's grasp of what facts are important, a deep understanding of social/cultural/political realities. And, as a special bonus, a great ability to capture the raggedy edges of hot sexual desire**. A scene on a roof during the famous city-wide 1977 blackout brings it all together.

"**In this book filled with humor, irony, and powerful social and cultural insights, 1970s New York comes vividly alive**. We see many things also that foreshadow the present. In a life filled with constant pitfalls, pratfalls, disappointments and setbacks, Robert Fairweather always keeps bouncing back up. More or less."

—ROBERT ROTH, AUTHOR OF *HEALTH PROXY*
AND CO-CREATOR AS WELL AS EDITOR
OF THE MAGAZINE *AND THEN*

"Dr. Robert Fairweather will never be known as a hero or a failure. But—despite the inordinate number of job opportunities, job losses, and the sheer and bizarre examples of bad luck—rather than hoping for some kind of good fortune, **I found myself rooting for *just one more description of yet another misfortune. I hope there'll be a sequel!*"

—ROBERT CENEDELLA, ARTIST, SATIRIST, BELOVED
TEACHER, SUBJECT OF THE FILM *ART BASTARD* AND
M. K. FLAVELL'S *THE AMERICAN ARIST AS SATIRIST*

"...reminds us that the fullness of life is determined by our willingness to embrace the journey's detours."

—EVA LESKO NATIELLO, *NEW YORK TIMES*
BESTSELLING AUTHOR OF *THE MEMORY BOX*
AND *FOLLOWING YOU*